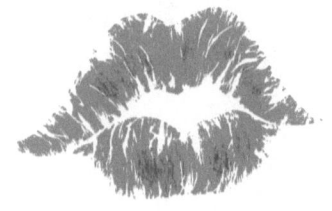

EVERNIGHT PUBLISHING ®

www.evernightpublishing.com

HOW LONG IS FOREVER?

DEDICATION

For my guy. You've always been my gooey hero.

HOW LONG IS FOREVER?

HOW LONG IS FUREVER?

Erin M. Leaf

Copyright © 2019

Chapter One

"Charlie, I have a towel for you," Eva called from the relative shelter of the front door overhang. She'd squished herself up against her house, hoping to keep from getting wet as she held the cotton fabric in front of her like a shield.

The man on the ladder spared a moment to fake scowl at her as the rain continued to pour down on him without mercy. A towel would do him no good at all until he finished his task and they both knew it, but she had to offer, right? It was only polite, after all. She held the towel out, half apologetically. Charlie shook his head at her, light brown eyes amused, then plunged his hands back into the clogged gutter.

Eva blushed and awkwardly tucked the towel under her arm. Embarrassment had her ducking her head. She wasn't sure if it was his expression, the water plastering every piece of clothing to his sculpted, muscular body, or her stupid comment, but it didn't really matter, did it?

"Sorry," she mumbled, knowing he couldn't hear her. She wished her dad were still alive to spare her this situation.

"I'll be done with this side in a moment, Eva," Charlie said, instead of yelling at her like another guy might. Then he coughed as dirty rainwater ran into his mouth. Eva cringed in sympathetic horror—those gutters were full of rotting leaves—but he shook his head like one of those dudes in a shampoo commercial, and all her sympathy went out the window as the spectacle of Charlie wet through to the bone registered against her retinas. The man was *fine*. He was more than fine, actually. He was the stuff girls' dreams were made of: all wet, flowing hair, solid muscle, and competence rolled up into a tight, teasing package of male awesomeness.

Eva bit her cheek, hoping the pain would jolt her out of her fixation on him, but all it did was make her wince. Charlie was a hell of a man, and he was here, right now, helping her out of a nasty situation.

"Girlhood crush, still ongoing," she muttered to herself, almost resentfully. If there was one thing she had always known in her life, it was that her father had loved her deeply and unconditionally, and she'd loved him back just as much. Growing up, that was all she'd needed. If he were still alive, he'd be the one up there on that ladder, and she wouldn't be stuck here staring at his best friend, Charlie Greenwood: wet as hell and just as hot.

Because the second thing that she'd always known in her life was that her dad's friend Charlie was probably the nicest man in the world. Certainly nicer than her stupid Uncle Albert, her mother's brother, who had made himself a nosy, leering pest ever since her mother had died a year and a few months after her dad.

Fuck cancer. And fuck sepsis. The infection had got her dad, and the cancer had taken her mother a year ago after he'd died. And so, after three horrible years of illness and hospitals and grief and railing against the unfairness of it all, Eva was alone, at the ripe old age of twenty-one, in the little house she'd inherited from her parents. And the gutters were clogged all to hell after the torrential rain this autumn. To top it all off, she hated heights, and that meant she needed help.

Enter Charlie, stage left, she thought, looking at his butt. His wet jeans clung in all the right places. She bet it made for a great handhold during sex, not that she'd know. She hadn't had time or inclination or opportunity for anything even remotely resembling a relationship, let alone a hookup in the past few years. Grief had a way of stopping life in its tracks. She hadn't even really begun life yet, anyway, before everything happened. She'd never been on a date. Never kissed anyone. She glanced down at herself, frowning at her generously-sized figure. *And it's not like anyone's ever lined up to play footsie with me, anyway.*

"Almost done," Charlie called out as he balanced on the ladder over top of the front walkway. Water cascaded down over his ridiculously ripped body while he dragged out huge handfuls of rotting leaves from the top of the downspout. Charlie was hands down the hottest man she'd ever met in her life, and she remembered well her utter dismay at age fourteen when she'd first realized that she'd have a crush on him forever. That knowledge was enough to squeeze her insides into a tight, uncomfortable knot whenever he was around, which was more often than she'd ever expected him to be now that her dad was gone.

You shouldn't be staring at his ass, she told herself, but she couldn't seem to help it. *He's probably twenty years older than you, you idiot,* the voice of reason in her head also said, but it didn't matter. Her gaze was firmly stuck on Charlie as he stretched out his arm again—insane muscles bunching under his sopping wet, faded green t-shirt. He reached into the clogged gutter to haul out a stinking, evil wad of decaying leaves and God only knew what else and flung the mess onto the ground. Of course, it was still raining. It was always freaking raining these days. The roof had started leaking into the living room above the bay window because the gutters were blocked. And because Eva's mom had been just as afraid of heights as Eva, no one had gone up there in several years to pull out the leaves. Charlie was who she'd had to call for help, and there he was right now. Soaking wet, right in front of her.

In all his glory.

Another thing Eva had always known was that she was abominably tall for a girl, and she definitely weighed too much, because the size sixteen jeans she used to wear didn't go up over her hips right anymore. And she didn't fit into normal sized bras. And most guys looked tiny to her as she stared down at them, so she had never managed a date, let alone a first kiss or any of the other normal things teenage girls did with boys. She'd been too large and too smart most of her childhood in comparison to the other girls at school, and then she'd been grieving, and so now here she stood, staring at Charlie because he was *so damned perfect* and she couldn't help herself. Charlie was the only man she knew who towered over her.

Eva was twenty-one years old, and everything about her life sucked right now, except her dad's best friend, who, at six feet five inches of gloriously muscled manhood, was *taller* than she was. Charlie made her feel positively petite. And he always came when she needed him. And that was why, as she stood under the eaves of the front porch, watching him throw stinking, awful gunk from the gutters onto the ground in the pouring rain, that she suddenly decided that enough was enough.

She was going to ask him for help with something far more embarrassing, and much more bothersome than her stupid gutters.

****

Charlie reached his arm into the gutter for the umpteenth time and cursed under his breath as he dragged out another handful of stinking leaves. He should've come here a month ago and cleaned out the damned things, but he'd forgotten, and now he was paying for it. He'd promised his buddy Phil he'd look after his wife Mary and their daughter Eva, and he'd done his best, but clearly, his best wasn't good enough. Phil had died, and then Mary had died, and Eva was the only one of the family left. She was barely grown and living in their house all by herself.

And now Charlie was here, in the rain, wet through to the bone. From the corner of his eye, he could see Eva watching him, fingers twisted in the towel she'd grabbed. She looked embarrassed and uncertain. She looked adorable. He gritted his teeth and made himself reach in and pull out another handful of stinking mess.

She's not for you, he thought to himself. *No. Nope. Not gonna look.* Eva had grown up into just the kind of woman he liked best but almost never met: tall, curvy, and gorgeous as hell. Even worse, she was ridiculously intelligent, and if there was one thing Charlie liked even better than boobs and ass, that was a woman with a brain. She'd managed to finish college *early,* despite her parents' illnesses and deaths. It had been difficult, but somehow, she hadn't broken under the misery of it all. He admired that. He admired *her*. If he were twenty years younger, he'd say he had a crush on her, but he was a grown man of thirty-five. Adult men did *not* crush on girls Eva's age.

"Do *not* look at her," he muttered under his breath, even as his eyes disobeyed him and shifted down and to the right. She stood under the front porch, hands crossed over her glorious boobs, curly hair in a wild mess around her shoulders. She'd slung the towel over her shoulder, and he could tell she'd used it to wipe rain off her face. He wanted to leap down off the ladder and toss *her* over *his* shoulder, towel be damned. He wanted to take her home and show her exactly what a man like him enjoyed doing to a woman like her, but she was his dead best friend's daughter, and that meant *hands off*.

"Looks like you got it all," she called out, eyeing the lack of water fountaining over the top of the gutter. "I've still got that towel for you." She uncrossed her arms and dangled it from her fingers. Of course she'd fetched a red towel. It was like waving a flag at a bull.

Frustrated, Charlie grunted, hand still in the freezing cold water now flowing through the gutter. *Maybe if I leave it in there a little longer it'll keep my dick under control,* he thought, but then conceded that it was a losing battle all around. Eva was just too damned enticing. He moved his hand around, mostly to buy himself some time to get his shit under control. The clog was gone. When he'd arrived, water had been gushing over the front of the bay window, and a leak had started inside on the ceiling. He'd be fixing that later after everything dried out. Now, though, the water was sluicing down into the downspout like it was supposed to, and he had no reason to stay up here on this ladder. Where he was safe. And fucking freezing.

"You coming down?" Eva called to him.

Charlie sighed to himself, then nodded, and then

he carefully stepped down the slick ladder. He should've worn his work boots, but he'd dashed out the door so quickly he hadn't bothered. His sneakers slipped on the bottom rung, but he caught himself and landed on the walk. He tipped the ladder back and drew the extension down. Eva's gaze bored a hole into his back. He had no idea what she was looking at. She'd seen him messing with ladders a hundred times.

"You want the towel now?" she asked.

He smiled wryly and tilted his head up as the rain continued to pound down on him. "I don't think your little towel is going to help much, Eva." He hefted the ladder and headed for her tiny garage, ignoring the water streaming down his face. It was a bit of a tight maneuver to get the damned thing down the stone steps on the side of the house, but he managed it. When he'd finished hanging it on the garage wall, he muscled the old, squeaky door closed and headed back up to the front of the house. Eva waited for him at the door. She looked adorable clutching the bright towel, but God help him, he wished she was wearing something less attractive. He'd always had a thing for women in sundresses, and Eva had a habit of wearing them often. The light cotton, though not form-fitting, hugged her curves in a way that left nothing to the imagination. He bit the inside of his cheek, hoping the pain would distract his libido.

"I can't believe it's still pouring down," Eva said, making a face at the sky. Even though she was under the overhang, it was raining hard enough to dampen her hair.

"Your curls are looking a little wild," he said, smiling. He couldn't help himself. He reached out and lifted the strand sticking to her cheek. She'd always had unruly, curly hair. He wanted to sink his hands into it and— *No. No, you do not,* he reminded himself, abruptly dropping the lock of hair.

"My hair is always a mess. You know that." Not seeming to notice his sudden irritation with himself, Eva sighed, impatiently pushing the mass of her hair over her shoulder. "It's been coming down for the past hour. And all day yesterday, too." She opened the door and held it for him. "Come on inside. The least I can do is feed you. I have a lasagna in the oven."

Charlie had just been planning on leaving so he could get home and dry off, *and stop imagining my friend's little girl naked,* he reminded himself, but lasagna was the magic word, and Eva knew it. He couldn't resist pasta. "You didn't have to make dinner," he said to her, following her into the house helplessly. The delicious aroma of sauce and garlic hung in the air, and he sniffed appreciatively. "Oh, God, that smells fantastic."

She flashed a grin at him.

Charlie smiled sheepishly. Eva's lasagna was to die for, probably because she used the same recipe her dad Phil had. Charlie had always loved his friend's cooking. His stomach growled embarrassingly, and she smirked. Charlie rolled his eyes as he paused just inside the front door, dripping onto the small square of ceramic tile. "I'm going to make a mess, honey."

Eva handed him the towel, not even blinking at the endearment that'd slipped out unintentionally. *Get a fucking grip*, man, he told himself.

"Go on into the bathroom. Take a hot shower. I can throw your clothes in the dryer while you warm up," she said.

Charlie looked at her for a moment, trying to wrap his brain around the idea of being naked in her bathroom, but then a shiver wracked his body. She was right, damn it. It might be summer, but the rain was cold, and now *he* was cold.

"Go on," she said, poking him until he moved away from the front door. She closed it behind them.

Charlie took the towel she held out and rubbed it over his face and hair. "Hang on." He toed off his shoes, then stripped his wet socks off his feet. The least he could do was minimize the damage as he walked through the house. He'd take off his pants and shirt, too, if he were alone and not sporting a massive erection. He hoped to God she didn't recognize the bulge pushing against his wet jeans. He knew she'd never had a boyfriend, never dated, so odds were she was still innocent about … stuff. He winced internally. That thought did *not* help calm him down in the least.

"I'll take those," Eva said, holding out her hands.

Charlie stared at her. "You want my dirty socks?"

She glared at him and snapped her fingers. "I want all of your wet clothes, Charlie."

Ha. If only. Charlie snorted and handed her the socks. She didn't seem to realize it, but she had the slightest hint of a blush high on her cheekbones. *Embarrassed?* he wondered. He smirked. She was the one who'd told him to strip.

"Go on to the bathroom. You know the way," she said, looking down at his feet. A tiny frown marred her brow.

Charlie shook his head, grimacing at the water that streamed off his hair. "Sorry," he said, looking at the droplets now decorating her tile entryway. He took off his shirt. That was safe, right? And the less clothing he wore to the bathroom, the less water he'd drip on the way there. When he looked up, he caught Eva staring fixedly at his chest. He held out his shirt. "Eva?"

"What?" A full-blown flush bloomed on her face. "Oh, yeah. Thanks." She took the shirt from him.

She was ogling my chest, Charlie realized,

surprised. He'd been noticing her for a while now, but he had no idea that Eva looked at *him* that way. In a sexual way. He looked at her face. She'd captured her lower lip between her teeth as if she were trying not to bite into a delicious candy bar. *And that's not a good thing,* he told himself, but it didn't help. His cock jerked despite the clammy, wet jeans he wore. The last thing he needed right now was for his erection to grow bigger. He had a difficult enough time controlling himself around her without trying to walk through her space with a giant hard-on that wouldn't fucking quit.

"Go on," she told him. She looked like she wasn't going to budge until he headed for the bathroom.

He sighed internally. "It won't take me long," he said aloud, striding through the comfortable living room and through the dining room. Like all the ranch houses built on this street, the floor plan consisted of a living room, a dining room, and a kitchen each leading to the other, and then a short hallway behind the kitchen that held three bedrooms and a bathroom. The house was small, but cozy. It was nothing like the airy, soaring modern cabin Charlie had built himself on ten acres of forest north of town. But he liked Eva's house. He'd liked it when it had been his friend Phil's house, and Eva had been just a child. Somehow, he liked it more, now. Eva had done something with it to make it her own, although he couldn't put his finger on exactly what.

"Hand me your jeans after you take them off so I can put them in the dryer," Eva said when he reached the bathroom.

Instead of answering, he closed the door most of the way and took off his pants, careful not to catch his dick in the zipper. He pursed his lips, wondering what she'd think when he didn't hand her any boxer shorts, then shrugged. What did it matter? She was off limits. It didn't matter what she thought. "Here you go," he said, slipping his arm with the sopping jeans through the cracked door.

She took them, and Charlie heard her open the basement door. He smiled wryly as he looked down at his erection. He hadn't wanted to come here and clean out gutters, but he'd made a promise to his friend. He hadn't wanted a hard-on, but now he had one of those, too. He turned on the water and stepped into the shower, rolling his eyes at himself when the scent of Eva's soap wafted up in the hot water, making his cock ache.

I'm not going to be able to cold shower this thing away, am I? he mused, then took himself in hand. He could jack off in ten seconds flat, especially in this shower, with Eva's stuff all around him. He groaned quietly as he recalled the blush on her face. She was twenty-one, but he'd bet his left ball she'd never touched an aroused man. Somehow, that thought just made him harder. He hissed as his fist squeezed the tip of his erection, and then his hips pumped once, twice, and it was all over. Jizz coated the pretty white tile of Eva's shower, and Charlie hung his head in the warm spray, panting and just a bit embarrassed. Had he ever come so fast in his life? He didn't think so.

"Fuck," he said a long minute later. His cock was still half-hard and sensitive, but at least now he could stuff it into clothing without injuring himself. At least, he hoped he could. Eva had a way of inspiring his body to new heights of stupidity.

"Hands off," he muttered, thinking of Eva and her gorgeous body and her pretty blush. "Fuck it all to hell."

Chapter Two

Eva stood by the dryer, clenching and unclenching her fingers. Charlie hadn't handed her any underwear, so he was either planning on wearing wet boxers, or he went commando. And after the display of wet, muscled male stripping off his shirt right the hell in front of her, she could barely function, let along contemplate the idea of Charlie wearing jeans without underthings.

"I mean, wouldn't the seams chafe his junk?" she mumbled, staring at the dryer as if she could make it work faster through sheer strength of will. She glanced up at the stairs. Right now, Charlie was completely naked and in her shower. She couldn't even imagine it. Since her parents had died, her shower had collected pink scrubbies and body lotions and hair products like a plague. And right now, Charlie, all six feet whatever of him, stood in the middle of all her girly stuff. Nude.

The contrast between her feminine items and his muscled, scruffy masculinity stuttered her brain, and she bit her lip as she waited for the dryer to do its work. She didn't even feel the cold cement under her bare feet. The basement was half-finished, and half-not. The clothes washer and dryer resided in the not finished part, so her bare toes curled under themselves on the cold cement slab where she waited. Heat sizzled in her core, and not for the first time she wished she wasn't so inexperienced.

"Eva?"

She whirled around, heart pounding.

"Do you have a pair of sweats I could borrow?" Charlie called down from the top of the steps.

"Oh my God," she breathed. Was he naked up there, at the top of her steps? God help her if he was. She hadn't expected him to finish in the shower so quickly.

She certainly hadn't expected him to saunter out of the bathroom with nothing to wear. Eva swallowed, then shook herself.

"Eva? You down there?"

"Hang on," Eva called back to him. The man was probably wearing a towel, right? Unsurprisingly, the image of Charlie with one of her pink towels slung low over his hips didn't help her at all. Not one bit. She glanced over the shelf where she'd put the last of her dad's clothes for donation, and grabbed the top bag. When she opened it, she nodded. His old sweats from college might fit Charlie. Her dad hadn't been quite as large as his friend, but beggars couldn't be choosers, and Charlie wasn't the kind of guy to complain about it. A pang of grief hit her, but she ruthlessly suppressed it. Her dad was gone. Charlie was here, alive and well and waiting for something to wear.

Eva grabbed the sweats and headed for the stairs, not surprised to see Charlie was no longer at the top. "Charlie? I have a pair of Dad's old sweats." She turned to the hallway, but he wasn't there, either.

"Thanks, Eva."

Eva nearly jumped out of her skin when Charlie put a hand on her shoulder. She whirled around.

"Hey. It's just me." Charlie smiled at her. "Relax."

Relax? Yeah, right, she thought, trying to get her voice to work. "Geez, you scared me," she finally said. Charlie's light brown eyes twinkled at her, and she dropped her gaze, then froze. *Oh. My. God,* she thought. Charlie really *was* wearing one of her towels around his waist. *I am never going to be able to unsee this.* A stray water droplet trickled down his ripped abdomen to the towel. A tattoo of a small bird in flight decorated his left pectoral. She stared at it fixedly. *He looks good in pink,* she thought inanely.

"You only have pink towels in the bathroom," he said, sounding amused.

Eva's skin caught fire. "Here." She thrust the sweats at him blindly, and turned before she lost all self-respect and grabbed for him. She wanted to rub herself all over his glorious skin. She wanted to grab his biceps and wrap his arms around her. She wanted him to hold her forever. A weird combination of lust and grief hit her. Charlie had been her rock for the past few years, and now her damned libido had woken up after a long drought, and of course he was the guy she couldn't shake from her head. Mouth dry, she tried to force herself to walk away, but she couldn't do it. Instead, she stared at the shelving unit that held her microwave in the corner of the kitchen as if her life depended on it.

"I'm decent now," Charlie said, voice low. "You can turn around."

He changed into the sweats right here? she thought, mind boggled. She turned around to find him hanging the wet pink towel over one of the kitchen stools.

"The lasagna will be ready in a sec," she said, grasping for something, anything, useful to say. The image of Charlie wearing her towel flashed through her mind in a delicious overlay of the current reality of him wearing her dad's too-small sweats. Neither vision was at all helpful to her peace of mind. Muscles flexed as he shifted his weight.

Charlie nodded. "Thanks." He leaned against the chair, crossing his arms over his chest.

Oh God, Eva thought, staring at the way his arm muscles bulged. *How in the world am I going to ask him for help with my stupid little problem? I can barely speak to him without staring at his chest.*

"So, how's your new job going? It's been, what? Six months now?" Charlie asked her. "Is everyone treating you okay?"

Eva swallowed and dragged her gaze up to his face. "Yeah." She had to stop and clear her throat. "It's been going okay." She shrugged. "I mean, it's not glamorous, but it's fine. Doing marketing for a hospital isn't my dream job, but whatever."

"Yeah, I hear you," Charlie said amiably. "You're doing okay for money?" He glanced around, as if checking for repairs to do.

He sounds like a dad. This is terrible, Eva thought, wondering if she should just forget her plan. "It's fine," Eva said. "My parents had good life insurance, as you know." She smiled weakly. "You're the one who talked me through the whole thing after they died." The oven timer binged, and Eva let out a breath. *Saved by the bell.* "There's our dinner." She bustled over to the stove and removed the lasagna. After slicing it and plating two servings, she steered Charlie into the dining room. "Beer?" she asked, heading to the fridge.

"Please," he said, already digging into the pasta. "Oh my God, Eva. Your lasagna just gets better and better." He closed his eyes while he chewed.

Eva looked at him and nearly dropped the drinks. Charlie had his head tipped back and he was half smiling as he chewed. He looked like a man relaxing after a bout of great sex. *Not that I would know,* Eva thought, thinking of her complete and total lack of a sex life, or a dating life, or any interaction with the opposite sex.

"Here," she said, surprised when her voice came out low and husky.

He opened his eyes and grinned up at her. "Sit down. Eat." He took the beer from her and kicked one of the other chairs out from the table. "You look tired. Or nervous. Or something."

Eva sighed. Of course she looked strange. She was nervous *and* tired *and* a whole lot of something because he was here, and he was gorgeous and perfect and she was a coward. She needed to follow through with her plan, but she had no idea how to bring it up.

Instead of talking to him, she began eating her lasagna. Maybe the food would help give her courage. Charlie tucked into the rest of his dinner, and Eva concentrated on chewing. But every so often she'd glance up and find Charlie looking at her with a strange expression on his face. After she'd finally cleaned her plate, she pushed it away. "What? You've been staring at me for the past ten minutes, Charlie."

He smiled sheepishly. "I was just thinking about how grown up you look these days."

Eva sucked her top lip between her teeth and bit it. Talk about a perfect opening. She wasn't going to get a better opportunity than this. She took a deep breath. "Actually, Charlie, that's something I wanted to talk to you about," she heard herself say. Her head buzzed, and she knew her hands had gone clammy. *If only he wasn't half-naked!* she thought, desperately wishing she had somewhere safe to put her gaze. Charlie didn't help matters when he leaned back in his chair, displaying his ripped chest perfectly.

"Oh?" he asked.

Eva's heart began a slow, hard pound. "Yeah, um—" She coughed when her throat closed up. "I need some help with something, and I was hoping you could, well, help," she said, smoothing her hands down her dress. She'd worn it because it was great at disguising her giant ass and highlighting her boobs, and she needed all the help she could get if she was going to convince Charlie to give her a hand.

"Of course," he said, leaning closer. "What is it? You know I promised your dad—"

Oh God, no. Do not mention my parents, Eva thought, face going hot. The help she needed had *nothing* to do with her mom or dad. Eva lifted a hand, stopping him mid-sentence.

"This doesn't have anything to do with him or my mom. This is more of a personal issue I need help with," she said nervously. She bit her lip again. Charlie's gaze flicked down over her, then up again and stopped at her mouth. Eva blushed harder. Why was everything in her life so freaking *difficult*? Why couldn't something, for once, be easy?

"Okay," Charlie said slowly, dragging his gaze up to meet hers. "What is it?"

Just say it. Just spit it out. What's the worst that can happen? He could say no, but disappointment never killed anyone, she told herself. *He won't laugh because he's not that kind of guy. Isn't that's why you're asking him in the first place? Charlie isn't just gorgeous; he's also nice.* Eva swallowed against the lump lodged like a brick in her throat. Her skin prickled. She didn't think she'd ever been so nervous in her entire life.

"It's okay, Eva," Charlie said, frowning slightly. "Just ask."

She gathered her courage. "I want you to show me how to have sex."

****

Charlie nearly choked on his next breath. *Show her how to—* He stared at her, but the words still didn't make sense. "Wait, what?" he asked, but Eva was still talking.

"I mean, I know I'm not the prettiest girl, and I'm not skinny, and I'm definitely too tall…" she was saying, but Charlie could barely register the words.

"Too tall?" he echoed as his heart banged on his ribcage. His gaze slipped from her face to her boobs, so beautifully packaged in her pretty purple dress. Almost unconsciously, he dropped his attention to where she twisted her hands together in her lap. Charlie knew exactly what she hid behind the soft fabric of her skirt: a full ass made for squeezing and perfectly curvy hips. "You're not too tall," he said, instead of what he was *really* thinking, which was: *What the actual fuck?* His lips felt numb. He wondered if the words he'd just spit out came out garbled.

"Then you'll do it?" she asked breathlessly. Her eyes stared into his, hopeful and innocent.

Jesus, God, give me strength. He was already shaking his head even as his cock thickened, *again*, inside the too-small sweatpants he'd borrowed. "Eva, no, you have no idea—"

She frowned at him. "I'm not a child. I know what I'm asking for. And I know it's a lot to ask given how I, well…" Eva trailed off, then began again. "Given me," she said, awkwardly waving a hand at herself.

Charlie swallowed, forcing himself to look at her face and nowhere else. If he kept staring at her breasts, he couldn't guarantee that he wouldn't just leap on her and start rutting like a wild animal. She thought she wasn't pretty? What the hell? "Your first time should be with someone you love, Eva. Someone your own age. I'm way too old for you," he said, proud that he sounded so reasonable. So *adult*. He watched her blush deepen, and then he felt like a total jerk for saying no, even though he knew he had to. He'd be even more of a jerk if he said yes. And seriously, how could he even contemplate this? He'd been her dad's best friend! He remembered her in pigtails!

"You don't understand, Charlie. No one wants

me. I'm too tall. I'm fat." Eva shook her head, looking angry now. "And I'm tired of never being good enough. I just want to get it over with. I want to feel like a grown woman."

"You're not too tall," Charlie said, confused. Too tall? Where did she even get that idea?

"Not for you," she said scornfully. "You're a freaking giant. But most guys don't want to go on a date with a woman who towers over them like I do."

Charlie struggled to make sense of this. "That's ridiculous. You barely come up to my chin. And you're not fat. Jesus, Eva." Charlie ran his hands through his hair. How did he get himself into these situations? This was a disaster. "You need to ask someone your own age out on a date. I know most of the time guys do the asking, but that's stupid, and I know you know that. Guys love it when girls ask them out." He nodded. If he were ten years younger, he'd jump on the chance to date her. Hell, even now his brain was supplying him with all the reasons why he could say yes, and he *knew* better. He was *not* going to screw around with Phil's little girl.

"I *have* asked, Charlie. I've asked more than one guy out, and every single one said no. Granted, that was before my parents died, but still. I *did* try." She emphasized her words with jerky hand movements. "It's hard to keep asking when you never get a yes." She stared down at the floor. She looked sad as hell.

Charlie's gut clenched. This ask of hers made no sense. "All the guys you asked are idiots." He ran a hand over his face. How the hell could he make this better? *Without* actually banging her hard and rough and all year long the way he wanted to? The idea of it had him grinding his teeth.

Eva snorted. "Yeah. I already knew that. That's why I'm asking *you*," she said, looking up again. Anger sparked in her gaze.

Anger is better than misery, Charlie thought, shifting uncomfortably on his chair. His cock pushed against the soft fabric of his borrowed sweats, reminding him that he was barely clothed. "I'm sorry. Maybe you just haven't met the right one," he offered, knowing that even as he said the words, she wouldn't listen. Hell, *he* wouldn't listen to those words if someone offered them. He sounded like an idiot.

Eva shook her head. "I'm already twenty-one, Charlie, and I haven't even been on a date. Not once."

Well, that just sucks. What the fuck is wrong with young people these days? Charlie sighed softly. "You realize that I'm an old man compared to you, Eva."

She looked him up and down. "You don't look all that old to me."

Charlie flushed. *Shit.* She could totally tell he had an erection. He wished futilely for a pillow.

"And I know I can trust you," she added, more softly. Her eyes were luminous. Trusting. "That's a lot more important than how much older than me you are."

Charlie felt like the biggest asshole on the planet. "I can't, Eva." He wanted to. God help him, he wanted to. But he could *not* take advantage of her, no matter that she was the one asking him. Phil would probably rise up out of his grave and punch him in the face if he touched her.

Eva sighed, then stood up abruptly. "Fine." She started clearing their plates. "I understand."

"Eva—" Upset, Charlie stood up, too, reaching out for her arm, but she avoided him. His erection deflated so fast he felt like his junk had whiplash. He hated disappointing her.

"No, it's okay. I don't want to talk about it." Eva's face was pink, and she wouldn't look at him as she loaded her dishwasher.

Shit. Charlie frowned, wishing there was something, *anything*, he could do to make her feel better. *Anything except have sex with her.* Just thinking those words sent a new frisson of heat sliding down his spine. He watched her bend over the dishwasher for a moment, gaze lingering on the curves of her hips, and then he glanced outside. The back gutters probably needed cleaning out. They weren't clogged yet, but it was probably only a matter of time. "I'll come back in a few days to clean out the other gutters, okay?"

Eva nodded, putting soap into the dishwasher. She didn't look up at him.

"And I'll come by to fix the drywall on the ceiling of your living room, too," he said.

Eva finally straightened up. She closed the dishwasher door with more force than was strictly needed. "You don't have to."

Charlie noticed that she carefully avoided looking him in the eye. "I want to. I promised your dad."

She frowned then. "That's nice of you." The buzz from the clothes dryer echoed up the basement steps. "I'll get your clothes." She hurried across the kitchen to the basement door.

Charlie watched her go, wishing he could go back in time and kick himself in the ass. If he'd simply come and cleaned out her gutters when he should've, none of this unpleasant conversation would've happened.

Chapter Three

Eva closed the front door behind Charlie and leaned back against it. She swallowed, and then banged her head on the hard wood. He'd dressed and headed out of the house in under five minutes after she'd handed him his dry clothes. She could tell he was embarrassed, but damn. There was no way he was as embarrassed as *she* was. "Well, you asked, at least. You go, girl," she muttered to herself. She'd asked. The worst had happened. The end. Now it was time to get on with her life.

And she did. For the rest of the week, Eva went to work, came home and ate dinner, puttered around the house for an hour or so, and then she went to bed. The problem was when she tried to sleep, her mind kept replaying images of Charlie's face when she asked her question, and embarrassment slowly gave way to frustration. It was an emotion she was used to, but that didn't mean she had to like it. Eva knew Charlie had been uncomfortable when she asked him for help, but she also knew that there'd been something else in his expression. Curiosity? Attraction? Whatever it was, it was enough to make her second-guess her decision to ask him and then leave him alone if he said no.

On Thursday, she sat at her desk during lunchtime, replaying the entire scenario through her head for the thousandth time. She grimaced as she bit through a carrot stick. *Maybe I hate him,* she mused, remembering how ridiculously hot Charlie had looked with water streaming down his body. *Maybe I love him. Either way, this sucks.*

"Hey, Eva. I have a favor to ask you," her friend Kyra said, propping a hip against her desk.

Eva blinked, banishing the images in her head

with relief. "What's up, Kyra?" She smiled at her coworker, but Kyra looked down, fiddling with the folders she held. Eva's stomach sank. She wasn't going to like this. Kyra was usually forthright and positive.

"So, uh, I was supposed to go on this dinner date tomorrow—" Kyra began, but Eva cut her off.

"No. Oh no." Eva glared at her friend, but Kyra avoided her gaze. "The one time you set me up on a blind date, all the guy talked about was his baseball card collection. Seriously. You promised me, Kyra." Eva grabbed another carrot and munched on it violently. "No. I don't even count it as a real date, and you know how desperate I am to pretend I'm normal."

"Please? I promised my mom I would meet this guy, but then Jonny asked me out again and we're leaving early to go to the shore." Kyra put on her best puppy-dog expression.

Eva glared at her. "This guy thinks he's getting *you*." She waved her hands at her friend. Kyra was five feet four inches of skinny gorgeousness, and Eva was … not. "I'm an Amazon giant compared to you. Guys run as soon as they realize that I'm taller than them." She glowered. "Once they can tear their eyes off my boobs, that is."

"You're not a giant. You're an Amazon warrior," Kyra said, grinning. "You could flatten me with one arm."

"I could flatten you if I sat on you, and your dog, too," Eva said, scowling. She was tall, and she was strong, thanks to her love of not sitting on her ass all the time, but she was also pudgy. None of that was anything a guy ever wanted to touch.

"Please? I'll owe you big time." Kyra crouched down. "My mother has been nagging me about this guy for ages, and I can't do it. I like Jonny."

Eva sighed. "Why don't you just tell your mom that you're dating Jonny? You've been with him for a year. This is getting ridiculous." She finished her carrots and stared sadly at the crackers that were all that remained of her lunch. She wanted a brownie. And chocolate milk. She sighed again. Eating healthy sucked.

Kyra stood up again and started pacing. "My mom wants to set me up with a nice Indian guy. I told her I wasn't ready to get married, but she doesn't believe me. She's been trying to set me up for the past six months with random guys her aunt or cousin or whoever told her about." She flipped her straight, dark hair over her shoulder impatiently, and Eva tried really hard not to envy her friend's shiny locks, but as usual, she failed. Her own hair was curly and unruly, and she usually wore it in a ponytail at work. When she didn't, her idiot boss liked to reprimand her for not being "professional and tidy". It was easier to tie it back.

"The arranged marriage thing actually sounds kind of useful, Kyra. It's like a safe dating service run by people who love you. I'd give my left arm for that," Eva said, thinking of her mom. She rubbed her chest at the familiar ache. That was the problem with her life: now that her parents were gone, she had nobody. It wasn't just that she wanted to have sex, she wanted to feel close to someone again. And Charlie was a good man. He was safe. She'd known him half her life. *No! You are not thinking about him, remember?* she told herself, feeling her face go hot.

"It's not a dating service, it's a cage." Kyra shook her head. "I know it looks great from the outside, but from where I am, it feels like someone tying my arms behind my back as they push me into a box." Her eyes flashed. "I hate it. I don't live in India. I've never lived in India. Just because my mother and father think it's a good idea doesn't mean it fits my life. Maybe for someone else, it's great, but not for me."

Eva pursed her lips. "What does this guy look like? And will he freak out when he sees me instead of you? His family probably set him up on this, too, you know. He's not expecting some huge white chick."

Kyra's face lit up. "So, you'll do it? Yes! Thank you!" She hugged Eva.

Eva fought her off as the corners Kyra's folders tried to drill a hole through her shoulder. "You didn't answer my questions."

"He looks like this," Kyra said, showing Eva her phone. "He's a dentist."

Of course he is. Dull as a doorknob. Eva grimaced, immediately ashamed of herself. She *wanted* to meet a nice guy. But nice guys were invariably dull, and there was nothing wrong with that, right? She ignored the little voice at the back of her head that reminded her that Charlie was both nice *and* interesting. She made herself look down at the picture. The guy looking up at her from Kyra's phone looked young and fit, and not particularly tall. He'd probably take one look at her and run the other direction. Guys like that never wanted to hang out with girls like her. "And what happens when I show up instead of you? I'm not Indian, I'm huge, and I'm not interested in marriage." *At least not with him,* she thought, very privately, as the image of Charlie wet from the rain flashed through her head, *again.*

"I'll let him know ahead of time. I have his number. It'll be fine," Kyra said, pulling up her contacts list on her cell. "He can't just bail, either, or his parents will give him a hard time. He *has* to show up, if only so he can tell them he did." She typed something into her phone, and then looked up, giving Eva a hard look. "And you're *not* huge. You're curvy. There's a difference."

"'Curvy' is what fat girls like to say to themselves to feel better about wearing plus sized clothing and horizontal stripes," Eva muttered.

Kyra rolled her eyes. "You outran me the last time we did that charity thing. So shut up."

I'm fat, but I'm fast. Ha. Eva slouched in her chair, slightly mollified. "You owe me, Kyra. You owe me big time."

"Yeah, yeah." Kyra slid her phone back into her pants pocket. "It's done. He's cool with it." She grinned at Eva. "Thank you. I'll make it up to you."

"He only *thinks* he's cool with it," Eva told her. How the hell did she get herself into these things? Oh, yeah. She was *nice. I think I want to swear off "nice" for the rest of my life.*

"Maybe you guys will hit it off!" Kyra said, walking away.

"In my dreams," Eva said, under her breath. She polished off her last two crackers and then packed away the wrappers from her lunch, feeling unaccountably depressed.

****

"He's late. Of course he's late," Eva muttered, poking a finger at her water glass. She was waiting in the cafe down the block from her work building, wishing she hadn't promised Kyra she'd do this. She had better things to do on a Friday night than go on a blind date with her friend's leftovers. Like water her plants. Or launder her socks. "Never again. I swear it."

She decided that she didn't really want to date anyone. She was fine by herself. Sex wasn't everything in life. She had a vibrator. And she was better off alone, right? It was safer. She wouldn't have to go on awkward dates where she had to worry about the guy being a secret serial killer. Although maybe she'd have to get a cat. That would complete her crazy single woman status.

"Hello? Eva?"

Eva looked up, ignoring the sudden butterflies in her stomach. *Show time,* she thought, steeling herself. The guy standing in front of her was thin, short, and staring at her as if she were an alien.

Why do I have a feeling this isn't going to go well? She tapped a finger on the orange she'd set down near her plate. The fruit was the agreed upon signal so her date would know how to find her. She took a deep breath and met his gaze. "Hey." She stood up and smiled. "I'm Eva Ruston. Nice to meet you." She stuck her hand out nervously. She *hated* this. If Kyra ever asked her for a favor like this again, she'd pretend she'd caught the plague and had to move out of the country. *Nothing* was worth this anxiety. She watched the guy's eyes roam over her body, and then he tipped his head ever so slightly up to meet her gaze. His expression wasn't encouraging.

"Oh, uh. Hi," he said, glancing down at the orange, then back up at her again. "You're Kyra's friend?" He didn't try to shake her hand.

Eva slowly let her arm drop. Her stomach had begun to hurt. "Yes. You're TJ, right?"

He swallowed. "I don't think this is going to work," he blurted out. "I'm sorry."

"Wait." Eva frowned. "What?" She thought of the appetizer she'd finally ordered when her stomach had growled so loudly the diners at the next table heard it. "But you just got here," she said, stupidly.

TJ flicked his gaze over her again, then started backing away. "Uh, you just don't look—" He cut himself off, looking embarrassed. "You're just, like, really tall. And … tall." He made a face. "And, uh. Wow.

I'm sorry. That didn't come out right." His cheeks turned dusky.

Eva stared. She had no idea what to say, except maybe, *fuck off, asshole*, but that wouldn't be very polite. Did she have to be polite at this point? She stepped back, stomach churning. "Look, I'm just here as a favor to Kyra."

Instead of replying, he just blurted out, "I'm sorry," and then turned on his heel and fled.

Eva blinked, watching as he practically ran out of the restaurant. "What just happened?" she asked, glancing uncertainly at the diners sitting next to her. Did they see what just happened? The woman gave her a sympathetic grimace while her partner talked on, oblivious, as most men were. *Yup. That lady saw the whole fucking debacle.* Embarrassment burned hot and horrible across Eva's face. She sat back down, staring at the remains of the mozzarella sticks she'd ordered. "Shit."

****

An hour later, Eva pulled onto the road leading to her house. The worst part about being stood up for a blind date was the awful, long commute home. She worked in midtown Manhattan, but lived in New Jersey, so she'd had to endure an hour and a half sitting on the bus, and then another half hour in her car, staring at the scenery going by while she replayed the horrible scene at the restaurant over and over again. She hadn't bothered staying to eat anymore. She'd lost her appetite. She was too tall. Too big. Too everything. She always had been. She might as well save herself the trauma of trying to find a guy. And she had a headache, anyway. She sighed in relief when her house came into view between the trees, and then her breath caught.

Charlie's truck sat in her tiny driveway, blocking

her usual parking spot in front of the garage.

"Fuck my life," Eva breathed as she pulled in behind his vehicle. She shut off her car, then leaned her forehead on the steering wheel. What was he doing here? Why tonight, of all nights? She supposed he was here fixing something, probably her living room ceiling. He was a *nice* guy. She didn't want a nice guy right now. She wanted ice cream, and comfortable jammies, and her bed, and a box of tissues. None of those things judged her based on how she looked.

"Shit," she muttered, pressing her forehead with her fingers. Her head really did hurt. She stayed hunched over for several minutes, breathing in and out until her heart stopped banging against her ribcage, and she was pretty sure she wasn't about to start bawling. Or barfing. "Come on, girl. Man up. What's the worst that can happen?" she asked herself, then snorted. She opened the car door and gathered her courage.

By the time she'd climbed the steps to her house, she'd almost convinced herself she wasn't about to have a nervous breakdown. It was only one terrible almost blind date, right? No big deal. She'd weathered far more trauma than a bad date. And this didn't count as a date, she decided. She still hadn't been on an actual date. *Right? Right.* Unfortunately, when she opened the door, her heart revved right back up again.

Charlie stood on a stepstool in her living room, arms above his head, patching the wrecked drywall on the ceiling. His hair had joint compound speckled here and there, and for some reason, none of the clothes he wore to her house ever fit him right. Today, he wore tight jeans with a rip in the right knee, and a blue t-shirt that was old, soft, and snug as hell over his pecs. He looked like he belonged on the cover of a romance novel, not in her stupid, tiny house.

Does he have to look so damn gorgeous? Eva wondered, humiliated all over again. She didn't *want* to be attracted to him, especially now. Not after he'd turned her down, and her blind date disaster. She really didn't want to deal with any of it anymore. She'd never felt so alone in her life.

"Hi, Eva," Charlie said, smiling at her over his arm. He was smoothing joint compound over a new patch on her ceiling.

"Hi, Charlie," she said, shutting her front door behind her. Her voice didn't waver, and that little victory calmed her nerves. "I had no idea you were coming over today." She dropped her purse on the sofa and then stood there, trying to decide if she should go cry on her bed after changing into her pajamas, or stand here pretending she was okay.

"Oh, I wanted to get this taken care of so you wouldn't have to deal with mold growing. It turned into a bigger job than I expected. I was hoping to be out of here before you got home," Charlie said, relaxing his arms.

Why? Because you don't want to face me after turning me down? Too awkward for you? Eva asked him silently. Bitterly. She couldn't bring herself to ask him for real. She toed off her shoes and left them in front of the door. Exhaustion dragged at her.

Charlie dropped the trowel he held into the rectangular mud pan full of compound, and brushed his hair back from his face. The motion left a streak of white along his cheekbone. "I've just finished." He looked around at the equipment he'd put on a cloth tarp. "I'll clean up and get out of your way."

Eva blinked, staring at the white smear on his face. Somehow, it softened his hotness level down from "holy hell I want to jump him right now" to "holy hell I want to hug him right now".

"Oh, okay," she said, too tired to come up with anything wittier. Her brain was fried, her libido was working overtime, and her heart was in the middle of a full-blown anxiety attack. Life just sucked, sometimes. All the time. Whatever.

"Eva? Are you okay?" Charlie asked, turning towards her with a concerned frown. "You look tired. Or upset." He pursed his lips. "Or both."

She just stared back at him mutely. *If I have to explain anything to him, I'm going to start sobbing,* she thought, very clearly, even as she felt tears well up. *Shit.*

Charlie walked over to her. "Hey. It's okay. Whatever it is, you're okay." He reached out and folded her into his arms. "You're okay. I promise. I'm here."

Eva thought about resisting, but it had been so long since anyone gave her a hug that she couldn't. She shuddered, sinking into his warm strength. He was hard and solid and everything she wanted, but it wasn't until he rubbed a thumb along her cheek that she realized she had tears on her cheeks. *I guess I'm crying after all.*

"What happened?" he asked after a moment.

Eva sniffed. He smelled like dust and wet plaster and *man.* He smelled like home, dammit to hell. "Nothing. Just a bad day." She pushed away from him, but he wouldn't let her go.

"Oh no, it's not nothing," Charlie said, holding her by the arms. "You don't walk into your house crying and tell me it's nothing."

She frowned up at him. "It's nothing you can help with, Charlie." What did he care, anyway? He'd turned her down. He didn't owe her anything.

Charlie nudged her over to the sofa, then crouched down in front of her as she sat. "Tell me." His light eyes glimmered more hazel than brown as he looked at her. He held her hands as if he were afraid she was going to fly away if he didn't anchor her to the ground.

He's like a dog with a bone. Eva sighed and explained as succinctly as she could. "I went on a blind date because I promised my friend Kyra I'd take her place. Her mom keeps trying to set her up. The guy took one look at me and ran for the door. He didn't even sit down."

Charlie shook his head. "I don't understand."

"What's not to understand?" Eva shook off his hands and grabbed one of the sofa's cushions, instead. She kneaded it to within an inch of its life. "I'm too tall, Charlie. And too fat. And I always have been and always will be. I've never been on a real date with someone who liked me. With someone who I liked back. I've never had a boyfriend, okay? It sucks. I'm tired and I'm lonely and I've never even had a first kiss." To her horror, she stared crying again. Why was she telling him this? *He'd* rejected her too. Could her life get any worse? "He told me I was too tall and too big," she said angrily, swiping her hand at her cheeks. "And you know what? I always will be. Nothing is ever going to change. A diet can only do so much. It won't make me shorter even if I do lose weight." She clutched the pillow like a lifeline. "I don't *want* to lose weight. I don't want to diet anymore. It sucks. If I'm not going to ever meet someone, then at least I'll have ice cream to hug."

"You don't need to lose weight, Eva." Charlie's expression slid from anger into something Eva couldn't interpret. "And you are *not* too tall. For God's sake, these guys you meet are fucking morons." He sat beside her and pulled her into a hug.

Eva blinked against his shoulder. Charlie had never cursed like that in front of her before, not that it mattered. His vehemence changed nothing. "You rejected me, too, remember?" she pointed out, still bitter over that. "I asked you for help, and you said no." She tossed the pillow aside.

"Because I'm too *old* for you, not because you're not the most gorgeous girl I've ever—" Charlie stopped in mid word. "Jesus," he muttered a moment later, looking frustrated. "You're not too tall. And you're sure as hell not fat. If those guys can't see that, then they don't deserve you."

Eva rubbed her face until the skin of her cheeks hurt. She couldn't seem to stop crying. "You *say* that, but no one else believes it. You don't even really believe it." She was sure of that. If Charlie had wanted her, he wouldn't have been able to say no to her so easily. She tried to stand up, but Charlie pulled her back down to the sofa.

"All the guys you know are stupid," he said.

"Well, then, I've never met one who isn't, except for my Dad," Eva said, implying that Charlie was stupid, too. *There. Let him chew on that.* She couldn't regret saying the words. She hadn't met a single guy who treated her well in her entire life except for the man her mom had married. Thank God for her dad. If he hadn't been such a good guy, she would've grown up thinking that all men were idiots. "Between the random assholes who call me a cow when I walk to work, the guys who run the other way when I ask them out, and the jerks who harass me when I'm trying to do my job…" She trailed off, too tired to keep arguing with him. "Whatever. I'm tired. Maybe I'll adopt a cat to keep me company." She stood up. Charlie didn't try to stop her this time. "Thanks for fixing my ceiling. I appreciate it."

Charlie stood, and Eva knew him well enough to tell that he was angry. The tension in his shoulders screamed it out to her. "The next time someone calls you some shitty word, you deck them, Eva."

"Really? That's your advice?" Eva rolled her eyes at him. "If I did that, I'd be out of a job as soon as that asshole manager comes over to leer at me again, and I'd be punching every other guy on the street each morning." She shook her head. "That's not how life works, Charlie. Fat women don't get to be angry. We're supposed to be funny and cheerful and oblivious." She ducked her head down and tried to walk past him, but he caught her up in a hug again. Eva bit the inside of her cheek, hard, but it didn't help. Tears rolled down her cheeks. Again. He smelled so damned good. And she felt safe in his arms because he was actually bigger than she was, and that was so fucking rare. God, she hated that he didn't want her.

"Shh. I've got you," he murmured, the jerk.

Eva wasn't sure if she wanted to punch him or cry harder. She was angry and upset and embarrassed. And she knew she looked like shit. When she cried, her skin went blotchy and snot ran out of her nose. She was *not* supermodel material, that's for sure.

"Just go home, okay, Charlie? I'm a mess tonight." She forced a smile. She had some pride, after all. "I'll be fine. It was just a really bad day. It wasn't even an actual date. The guy didn't hang around long enough for it to be a date. He was late anyway, so I ordered mozzarella sticks, which were delicious, and now I'm home and tired and I just want to go to bed. It wasn't all that bad of a day. Really." She hoped he believed her because she couldn't keep this up. She was going to die of mortification if he stayed. How much humiliation could a girl take?

He tipped her chin up. "So you went on a blind date to help your friend, and not only did the guy bail, he insulted you after getting there late. And then you ate all by yourself, *and* paid for your dinner. By yourself."

Eva's face burned. "Thanks a lot, Charlie. I really didn't need a recap about how pathetic I am." She pushed at him. How could he? Even as anger surged through her, she couldn't help but notice how damned *solid* he was. Pushing him felt like pushing at a wall—hard and immovable. *Except, walls are cold, inanimate objects and he's anything but,* her libido whispered to her. She flushed as her palms tingled. She pushed at him again. This was the closest she'd ever been to him aside from brief hugs here and there.

"That's not what I meant." He sighed and let her go when she kept shoving at him, but he didn't let her go far. He grasped her wrists gently. "You are *not* fat. You are *not* too tall. You are magnificent." And he smiled. "You are one of the strongest women I know." His thumbs rubbed circles on her pulse points.

Eva stared at him, trying not to lose her anger. Anger made her strong. Anger made her less likely to start crying again. But of all the things he could've said, *magnificent* wasn't what she'd expected. "I'm not strong." She felt tears well up again, damn it all to hell. She felt tired and trembly. If he weren't holding onto her, she would've collapsed already.

He shook his head. "You *are,* Eva. You graduated college early. You dealt with your parents' illnesses all by yourself. After they passed away, you found yourself a job in the city and kept on going. You keep on living and trying things and challenging the world, despite all of the shitty stuff that's happened, and despite the awful people who keep trying to pull you down."

Eva chewed on her lower lip. Was this the same man who'd turned her down? "If I'm so awesome, why did you say no to me, too? I asked you for—" She broke off, hardly able to believe she was pursuing this. *But if I don't ever try, nothing will happen,* she thought, taking a deep breath and continuing. "I asked you to kiss me. To teach me. I told you no one else would. And if you don't think that was humiliating for me, you're dumb as a rock."

"A rock, hmm?" Charlie grinned, but then the smile slipped away. "Eva, all my life I've felt like a giant. The women I've dated were so small and fragile, and it never worked out."

He would *understand, and that makes it worse,* Eva thought. "Then you know what I'm talking about. You know what it's like to feel as if there's no one who could ever fit you. You know what rejection feels like," Eva said, aggravated all over again. "And you still said no to me." How was this her life? Was she doomed to be forever chasing after guys who didn't want her?

"Because if I say yes, I wouldn't be able to stop," he whispered, eyes dark.

Eva frowned. What the hell did *that* mean?

"Oh, hell. Don't look at me like that, Eva," he said. He still hadn't let go of her wrists. He was so hot, his hands felt like brands on her skin.

"What do you expect? I've got nothing to lose, Charlie. I've hit rock bottom here." Eva wished he would let her go. She wanted to bury her misery in ice cream. "Let me go. If you don't want me, just let me go."

Chapter Four

Charlie stared at her while his body warred with his mind. Her wrists were soft and warm in his hands. He wanted nothing more than to kiss her and hold her and make sure nothing ever hurt her again, but he knew if he let himself take her in his arms again, he'd be lost. If he kissed her, he'd never be able to let her go.

"Let me make you dinner," he said, trying to find a way to help her without breaking every last one of his rules about what you did and did not do with your best friend's daughter. "You must be hungry if all you ate were a couple of mozzarella sticks."

She blinked at him, and he could see the exhaustion on her face. "Is this some sort of trick question?"

"No," he said immediately. He tugged on her wrists, steering her through the living room towards her bedroom. "No tricks. I cook, you eat. Why don't you put on something more comfortable?" He nudged her into her room and stood in the doorway. "I'm not the best cook, but I think I can manage an omelet."

She turned. "Eggs sound good," she said, sounding confused. And tired.

Charlie hated how tired she looked. A twenty-one-year-old shouldn't look that exhausted, but then she'd had a lot on her plate for the past four years. "Come on out to the kitchen whenever you're ready. I'll get started."

He walked away. He had to. If he'd stood there any longer, he would've gone into her room and stripped off her clothes and taken her to bed. There was something about a tired woman that stirred every last one of his protective instincts. And when that tired woman was Eva, well... He barely had control of himself on a good day around her, let alone one where she was hurting.

He headed for the kitchen and raided her refrigerator. Fifteen minutes later he had all the fixings for an omelet lined up on the counter. A noise behind him had him pivoting, but it was the sight of Eva in worn, tight sweats and a baggy t-shirt that made him swallow. She'd taken him at his word and dressed comfortably. How was she to know that the sight of a woman with her hair messy and feet bare was exactly the look he most loved? That level of casual implied trust, and there was nothing sweeter than a woman who trusted her man to take care of her. *Except I'm not her man, and I never will be*, he thought, surprised at how much that bothered him.

"Looks yummy, Charlie," Eva said, still sounding subdued. She sat at the breakfast bar and propped her chin in her hands. She'd scrubbed her face clean of makeup, but it didn't make her look one bit less desirable. Eva was all woman at any time of the day or night.

Wait a second. Woman? She's not a woman— she's Phil's daughter. She's only—

Charlie's thoughts crashed to a halt. Eva *was* a woman. She was twenty-one years old. And after nursing her parents through their final days, no one around could claim she wasn't an adult. He stared at her for a moment while he wrestled with himself. His gaze slipped down to her breasts. She'd taken off her bra, and all that curvy goodness loose inside her t-shirt was enough to make him lose his fucking mind. He cleared his throat. "One omelet, coming right up. Anything in particular you want in it?" He turned to the stove and began whipping two eggs in a bowl.

"Everything you have there is good," Eva said,

looking at the veggies he'd chopped.

Charlie prepared her dinner, concentrating on making it as perfect as possible. When had he begun to see her as a woman instead of as a girl? And what did it matter, anyway? She was still hands-off to him. He was too old. She was Phil's daughter. He had morals. He expertly slid her eggs onto a plate, then presented it to her with a flourish. He'd already set out drinks and toast. "There you go. Perfection on a plate, if I do say so myself."

She snorted. "Bit of an ego there, eh?"

"I only boast when it's true," Charlie said, secretly pleased he'd made her smile, even if just for a moment.

Eva rolled her eyes at him, so Charlie grinned and made himself an omelet with the leftovers. When he sat down next to her with his food, she leaned into him. He put an arm around her shoulders without even thinking about it. She felt perfect there. Charlie fought to keep it casual, but his body knew what it wanted, and it wanted Eva. He angled his hips slightly away so she wouldn't see his erection pressing up against the front of his jeans. Seemed like he *always* had a hard-on around her these days.

"I'm so tired," she murmured after a moment. To his relief, she'd managed to eat most of her food. "I wish I could sleep for a year."

"Drink up. You need hydration." Charlie nudged her sweet tea towards her as he inhaled his food. He hadn't stopped to eat before coming over here, and he'd put in a full day at his construction site working on the latest order. "You had a rough day."

"I've had a rough year. Years." She drank half the glass in one go. "Why do guys suck, Charlie?" she asked in a small voice.

HOW LONG IS FOREVER?

He sighed as his heart lurched in his chest. He hated that she was so miserable, and he especially hated that it was because so many men were such a bunch of fucking assholes. "They don't all suck, Eva," he said, hoping she believed him. She needed a bit of positivity right now. "You've just been unlucky enough to meet only the idiots."

"The idiots are loud and obnoxious. And there are a lot of them," she said pointedly, sounding a bit more like herself.

Charlie chuckled. "True." He finished his dinner and watched Eva play with the last few bites of her food. He could tell she felt better, but he also knew she didn't really *want* to feel better. *And I don't blame her. Being angry is sometimes the only way to get through a rough time.*

"Why won't you at least kiss me?" Eva asked suddenly, turning her head to look at him. Her hazel eyes shone green in the setting sunlight slanting through the kitchen window.

Fuck. Charlie went still. Her gaze felt like it had pierced through to his soul. "Because I'm too old for you, Eva. And you're my best friend's daughter." He tried, God help him, but he couldn't keep himself from looking at her mouth. She had the most kissable lips he'd ever seen on a woman. And the most startling, soft hair. And amazing skin. And he couldn't forget her brains. *Stop it,* he admonished himself, forcing his gaze up to her eyes.

"My dad died over two years ago. Your best friend is dead," Eva said softly. She was no longer crying. She looked like a woman who knew her allure, no matter how strongly she denied it. "And I'm no longer a little girl."

Charlie swallowed against the lump in his throat.

How could a man feel grief and lust at the same time? Phil would kill him if he were alive to know what Charlie was thinking about Eva, his little girl, wouldn't he? The daughter he'd never expected to have. Phil had loved her with all his heart. Charlie had to respect that. "Eva—" he began, but she cut him off.

"No." She stood up and pushed her plate away from her. "Forget it. I'm done asking. I don't want a pity kiss, and I'm tired of arguing with you." Eva frowned, then kneaded her forehead with her thumbs. "I'm sick of begging for crumbs. I deserve better. You know the way out, Charlie." She pivoted on her heels and strode to her room.

Charlie watched her for a split second, then rushed after her. He knew he'd regret this even before he started moving, but he couldn't seem to help himself. He wanted her with a desperation that made no sense. He tried to tell himself that he hadn't even *thought* of her in a sexual way until she'd asked him to sleep with her, but that was a lie. Even so, it felt as if that request had opened wide a door in his mind and his body, and now all he could think about was her. Eva. Her curvy body and sassy mouth were made for sex, and he knew she'd be so damned tight and wet and hot... He caught her arm just beneath the elbow and spun her around right before she entered her room. The tiny hallway where they stood felt like it had run out of air. He couldn't breathe. He couldn't *think.* "You're playing with fire, Eva. When you do that, you get burned."

She laughed, but it wasn't a happy sound "You're spouting clichés, Charlie. Go home."

Instead of listening, he pressed her up against the wall. She didn't resist. "I'm too old for you," he bit out, even as he leaned in. "You deserve better." Even as he spoke, he sighed at the feel of her against him. Her body fit his perfectly in all the right places: thighs against his, belly against his cock, breasts against his chest. He'd never had the pleasure of holding a woman this tall and strong and curvy, and he wasn't sure he'd ever be able to forget how Eva felt. He just barely kept himself from grinding his erection into her delicious softness.

What are you doing? This is Phil's daughter, he told himself, but he didn't let go. He *couldn't* let go. *Just let me hold her for a minute. Just for a second, and then I'll be good. I promise,* he swore mentally, to no one at all. He couldn't even fool *himself* at this point.

"How old are you?" she asked, eyes glittering defiantly. She wasn't the least bit intimidated by him. It was a shocking turn-on. Women had always found him just a bit overwhelming. The fact that she didn't... His thoughts ran off into a jumble of arousal and need.

"You're always saying you're too old for me. How old are you exactly?" Eva asked.

"What?" Charlie asked, trying to make sense of her question. He glowered down at her, but thank God she didn't look frightened. Charlie'd had to deal with that more than once in his life when he got up close and personal with a woman, and he hated it. He hated that his size intimidated women. *But not Eva,* a tiny voice whispered in the back of his head.

"I mean, I know you're younger than Dad was," she continued as if he wasn't looming over her. "But how *much* younger? Wasn't your older brother friends with him first?"

Charlie frowned down at her as his brain finally figured out what she was asking. Why did she want to know this now? "Yeah, he was, before my brother Frankie died, but it doesn't matter. I'm still too old for you."

She looked at him for a long moment, making no

effort to get away. "Then what are you doing, Charlie?" she finally asked, in a voice so soft it sent shivers down his spine. "What are you doing *here* with *me*?" She emphasized her words with the slightest wiggle of her hips against his erection.

Charlie growled inarticulately under his breath. He had no answer for her. Instead of even trying to organize his thoughts and put them into words, he blew out a breath. Eva looked up at him, rumpled and sweet and so alluring he couldn't think at all anymore. He gave up wrestling with his mind and conscience and leaned in to press his mouth to hers. She gasped, and he swept his tongue along her lower lip. She tasted like salt and sweet tea and woman. She tasted like home.

I'm so fucked, he thought, but he didn't stop. He just kissed her again.

****

Eva gasped as Charlie's lips met hers. He felt big and strong and so fucking hot she could barely think *before* he kissed her, but now her brain went nuclear— sparks in all directions. She mindlessly scrabbled at his arms and sank her fingers into his shoulders. He didn't flinch. He didn't stop or push her away. He took everything she threw at him like a solid wall of awesomeness.

"Beautiful," he breathed, breaking for air.

She sucked in a breath, but before she could say anything, he kissed her again. He hauled her up against him, moving her as if she weighed nothing at all. Eva squeaked, but Charlie didn't let go. He kissed her deeper, sweeping his tongue along her lips and then into her mouth as if he would die if he couldn't taste her. When he finally lifted his head, she swallowed, hard. She had to *look up* to see him, and wasn't that something else. *Holy what the fuck. Be careful what you ask for,* she thought hazily. Her lips tingled. Her *pussy* tingled, and he hadn't even gotten to second base.

Charlie didn't speak. He looked at her with eyes gone dark and hot. He didn't let go. He loomed over her like a beast, and Eva shivered and dug her fingers into his muscles. He didn't even seem to notice. She liked him like this. She liked him in every way it was possible for a woman to like a man.

"Wow," she whispered. Her lips felt swollen. Her tongue felt stupid. She bit her cheek so she wouldn't beg him for more.

"Is this what you wanted?" he finally growled, aggressive and so damned *male* she shivered.

Eva licked her lips. "Yes." It was her first kiss, and it was *everything* she'd ever wanted: a man who wasn't afraid of her brain or her size or her strength. Charlie had no idea how rare that was. She gathered her wits. "More," she said. "Please."

Charlie inhaled sharply, eyes on her mouth. "God help me." And then he lowered his head.

Eva trembled, expecting his lips on hers again, but instead, he kissed down her jaw to her throat. His mouth was hot and soft and ridiculously gentle.

"You smell like citrus," he said, voice low and rumbly. "I want to eat you up."

Good lord. Eva moaned, then hissed when he scraped his teeth along the sensitive skin near her ear. "Don't stop," she said, finally getting the courage to slide her fingers up into his hair. He still had some dried flecks of joint compound in it, and she smoothed it out of the strands as he kissed her again. For the first time, she tried to kiss him back. When her tongue met his, he groaned.

"Yeah. That's it, honey." Charlie bit her lip, then soothed it with his mouth.

Eva found herself writhing against him, trying to

get closer. *No wonder people do crazy things for love,* she thought, wishing she could crawl inside him. His body pressed hard and heavy against hers, and he didn't even budge as she wriggled. Something hot and thick pressed against her abdomen, and with sudden clarity, she realized it was his erection. Charlie was aroused. The sudden knowledge was enough to jerk her out of her sensual reverie. "Oh my God," she said, voice breaking. "Oh my God."

"Not God, Eva. Just a man." Charlie kissed her again, sliding his hands up her body. One slid around her right breast, flicking the nipple. She hadn't bothered with a bra, and clearly, he'd noticed. He cupped her and rolled his hips into her in a slow facsimile of fucking. "You're so fucking gorgeous. Lush. Perfect." His fingers teased her nipple into a tight, aching point. "Fuck. I want you so bad. I can't stop touching you. Make me stop, Eva. Tell me no."

Stop? Like hell I will, she thought, urging him on with her body. Eva's skin prickled as pleasure shot from her breast to her clit. Her pussy throbbed, swollen and wet. She wanted more. So much more. She'd be totally okay if he wanted to go all the way with her right now. She wished he would.

"Please, Charlie," she said, shocked when her voice came out soft and breathy. The best part about all of this was that she *knew* Charlie. She'd been half in love with him for years, and she could easily slip the rest of the way down that particular rabbit hole. She slid her hands down over his waist, then up under his tight shirt. His skin was silky smooth. Muscles contracted under her fingertips.

"I shouldn't be doing this," he muttered, even as he kissed her again. "I'm just going to hurt you."

"No, you won't." Eva wound a leg around his

thigh. His cock was so hot it felt like a brand against her belly. She couldn't even imagine what it might feel like *inside* her. "I *want* you to do this, Charlie," she said, just in case he got the ridiculous idea that he was forcing her into it. "I asked you for this, remember?"

Charlie growled again, sucking on her neck. It hurt. It felt divine. Eva sank her hands into his hair and made fists as he ravaged her neck. The harder she pulled, the wilder he became, so she gripped his hair with all her strength. When he bit down, she gasped, trying to get some friction at the juncture of her thighs. If he would just move his leg a little bit to the left...

He slid his hands down and cupped her ass, hauling her up against him. Eva ended up grinding down on his thigh. She shuddered, head falling back. She'd fingered herself to orgasm a hundred times, but it had never felt like this. *Nothing* in her life had prepared her for this.

"Charlie, please," she begged, not sure what she was asking for. "I need more."

He kissed her again, then slowly lowered her down and grasped her wrists. "Eva," he said, whispering her name into her ear. "Shh, baby."

"Wait, no," she said, trying to get closer again. Why was he pulling away? She was so *close.*

Charlie panted, his forehead on her shoulder. "We have to stop."

Eva shook her head. "No, we don't. I know you, Charlie. I picked *you* for my first time." She tried to pull her hands free, but he tightened his grip, and damn it all to hell, the restraint excited her even more. She loved that he was strong enough to handle her. No one else had ever even tried. "Please. I'm not a child anymore. I'm not just your best friend's daughter, and you know it."

Charlie sighed, sounding as frustrated as a man

could be in this situation. "No. Eva, stop." He set her away from him.

Eva stared at him, unable to believe he'd stop *now*. "Wait. Are you serious?" She stared at him. His mouth was swollen. She tentatively touched her lips. So was hers. Her fingertips did nothing to cool the heat, but she liked the way Charlie watched her as she touched herself. "You can't be serious," she said, half teasing, half begging. She bit down on her finger just to watch his breath hitch.

He grimaced, looking pained, and then he kissed her again, very gently. "I'm serious. This is wrong." He looked regretful. "I'm so sorry, Eva. This is all on me."

This is bullshit. Eva didn't want gentle. She wanted big and strong and fearless. "Charlie, you don't—"

He cut her off. "I know better than to do this." His expression tightened. "I can't. Eva, I'm sorry." He thrust his hands into his hair and tugged. "God! I'm such an idiot." He cupped her face. "I'm so sorry."

"This was my first kiss, Charlie," she said angrily, not in the least pleased with his sudden attack of guilt. "You realize that, right? And you're ruining it." She shook off his grip and stepped back. He was making this all about *him,* and that just pissed her off. How dare he pretend to comfort her after her truly shitty day, and then *finally* kiss her, and then back off like she'd caught the plague or something? "I'm a grown woman, and I wanted you to kiss me. I *asked* you to kiss me, remember? Remember the other day when you stomped off?"

"This has nothing to do with you, Eva, and everything to do with me being a jerk," Charlie said in a low voice.

She snorted. *Well,* that's *certainly true.*

"You're a beautiful, intelligent woman, and I stepped over a line I swore I would never cross." He ran a hand through his hair.

Eva's anger erupted. "Get out." She pointed down the hall. "I can't even look at you right now, Charlie." How dare he act like he was the only one making the decisions here? "I'm an adult. I've been an adult from the first moment my dad got sick, and you know it. And I know what I want," she said, voice cracking. Her finger shook, and she let her arm drop. She wanted to slap him. "Right now, I want you gone."

Charlie nodded, stepping back. "I'm so sorry." He turned and walked towards the kitchen, then paused. "I'll be back on Sunday to do the gutters out back, if that's okay with you?"

Eva gritted her teeth. If she could, she'd rip the damn things off the house and burn them, but she had to be sensible. She still needed his help, even if just looking at him made her want to crawl into a hole and never come out. Her face burned, and the lump in her throat wouldn't budge, no matter how much she swallowed. She twisted her fingers together tight enough to hurt. She only had to keep from crying for another minute. Maybe two, tops.

"Eva?"

"Fine," she said instead of hurling something at his damn head.

Charlie nodded, short and sharp. "I'm really sorry."

Eva scowled at him. She didn't want to hear apologies.

Charlie sighed, shoulders tight. He still had plaster in his hair. Eva suppressed the urge to go to him and fix it.

"Sunday, then," he finally said, then turned and

walked away.

Eva clung to the edge of her bedroom door. As soon as she heard the front door shut, she went into her room and flung herself facedown on her bed, tears hot on her face.

It took her a long time to fall asleep that night.

Chapter Five

On Sunday afternoon, Charlie pulled his truck into Eva's driveway behind her car, then cut the engine and sat there for at least ten minutes. *Coward,* he told himself, staring at her house. When he'd left the other night, he'd had to move her car first, then back his out, and then park hers again, all while knowing she was probably crying her eyes out in the bedroom right above the garage. The entire process added fifteen minutes to an entirely hideous situation, and he had no one to blame but himself for the whole thing. Right now, though, the sun was shining, and clearing the back gutters shouldn't take long. He still couldn't get himself to move. He'd spent all day Saturday trying not to think about how fucking perfect Eva felt in his arms.

He'd failed.

In desperation, he'd gone for a brutal ten mile run late Saturday night, and now he was paying for it. His legs hurt. His feet hurt. And worst of all, his mind continued to bombard him with images of Eva: hair down, no bra, sass and fire in her eyes. When he smothered the images, her voice echoed in his head instead, reminding him that she was as intelligent as she was beautiful. Trying to distance himself from her emotionally seemed to be a losing battle.

"And sitting here isn't going to fix anything," he muttered irritably. He sighed, then got out of his truck. *I'll go right to the backyard and get the gutters done, then get the hell out of here,* he promised himself. *No kissing. No* thinking *about kissing.*

He unhooked the tailgate and pulled out his ladder. He could've used Eva's equipment, but then he'd have to ask her to open the garage door, and the less time spent interacting with her the better. He already had an erection. He'd had an erection since he'd got in his damn truck to come over here, damn it to hell. He couldn't get the idea that making love with Eva would be as close to heaven as he could get, and he knew he was going to hell for it. You did *not* mess around with your friend's daughter. Not ever, no matter how perfect she was for you. Not even if she asked you for it. And you especially didn't mess around with her when your friend was dead. That made everything a thousand times worse, because it was on him to keep Phil's daughter safe. No one else was going to do it. A pang of grief hit him right in the chest. Phil had been there for him when his brother had died years ago, and now Charlie would never be able to repay him, except through Eva. *Which means I'm supposed to take care of her, not fuck her,* he thought darkly. *I shouldn't even be* thinking *about fucking her, you old pervert.*

Charlie hefted the ladder over his shoulder and headed up the stone steps and around the house. The edge of it bit into his neck, but he didn't readjust it. He deserved the pain. He walked slowly, careful not to smack the house with the awkward thing, but when he reached the corner, he frowned, stopping just out of sight of the back yard. Angry voices carried around the building.

"How many times do I have to say 'no' for you to understand me?" Eva was saying. Her words were hard and clear. There was no mistaking the irritation in her tone. "No. A thousand times no, Albert. You are not welcome here. Please leave."

Albert… I know that name. Charlie leaned the ladder against the house as he racked his brain, trying to remember the identity of the man. Eva would be able to tell him, but he wanted to understand what was happening before he interrupted the conversation.

"I promised your mom I'd help you out, Eva," the man said. "I can't do that if you don't let me."

"I wouldn't let you do anything for me if you were the last man on Earth," Eva retorted. "If you wanted to help me, you could've tried not being an asshole when Mom died. You didn't even come to her funeral! What kind of brother does that?"

Ah. Mary's younger brother, Charlie realized, not pleased with the knowledge. Phil had hated the man, and hadn't allowed him in the house during their marriage.

"I was away on business. You've got to cut me a break," Albert said.

"I don't have to cut you anything. You're supposed to be my uncle, not some old creeper," Eva said, her voice rising.

And now I know why Phil hated him. The little bastard doesn't know how to take no for an answer, Charlie thought, annoyed for Eva's sake. He'd never met the guy, and from what he heard now, he hadn't been missing much. *After everything she's been through, she shouldn't have to put up with this shit.* Charlie didn't like the whiny sound of the guy's voice, uncle or not. And he didn't like anyone harassing Eva.

He walked around the corner, then stopped. Eva stood with her hands fisted by her sides. She looked like she'd been reading on her small patio, because a discarded paperback rested on the chaise lounge and a tall glass of iced tea sat on the small glass table next to the seat. She wore cut-off shorts, a pretty orange halter-top, and a wide brimmed straw hat. She looked young and pretty and pissed.

No, not pretty. Pretty is too ordinary a word. She looks fucking phenomenal, Charlie thought, staring at all the delicious skin on display. She looked like she belonged in a photo shoot. She also looked irate. Before he could say anything, the man standing in front of her grabbed her arm and forced her closer.

Fuck, Charlie thought, as anger welled up. How dare the little weasel put hands on Eva? Charlie started forward just as he caught sight of another man standing just behind Albert. The dumbass was grinning like a fucking donkey. Neither man saw him, but Eva did, and her expression told Charlie just how upset she really was.

"I'm just trying to take care of you," Albert said, oblivious to the world of hurt about to descend on his head. He was shorter than Eva, and fat, and ugly. His friend was only slightly taller, and he'd positioned himself so that Eva couldn't easily back up.

"By hitting on me? Do you know how gross that is, Albert? You're my uncle, for God's sake. Have some self-respect," Eva retorted angrily. She swung her arm around, breaking his grip. When she stepped back, she landed in the other guy's arms. "What the—" She struggled as the other man grabbed her upper arms. "Let me go!"

He jerked her closer to him. "We just want a little compensation for coming to visit you."

"You're crazy! Get your filthy hands off me!" Eva wrestled with him, then broke free, and then she used her momentum to punch the man in the head. "You wouldn't deserve compensation even if you had done something useful. Get out of my yard!" She raised her fist again.

He staggered back, hand on his ear, then hissed. "You fat bitch! You should be grateful we're actually paying attention to you! No one else will, with hips like that. And you're too fucking tall." He reached out as if to hit her, and Charlie saw red.

"Get the fuck away from her." Charlie strode forward, pissed. Eva looked at him, and the combination of anger and frustration in her eyes nearly broke his heart. "Are you okay? Eva?"

She nodded jerkily, emotion flashing across her face. "I'm fine." She turned to her uncle. The other guy had circled around to stand near him. He looked younger than her uncle, but just as smarmy. His belly rolled out over his pants, and Charlie could tell he liked to hit the beer a little too heavily.

"Who the fuck are you?" the guy asked belligerently.

Charlie ignored him. *I wouldn't be surprised if these jokers aren't half drunk right now,* He thought, looking at their glassy eyes. "Did they hurt you before I got here?" he asked Eva quietly. He touched her arm and was gratified when she moved closer to him.

"No," she said, and then she sighed. "Depends on your definition of hurt."

Charlie scowled.

"They've been here for a half hour, uninvited. They interrupted my day so they could get their rocks off harassing a woman," Eva continued. "But I'm fine. They were just leaving." She turned to glare at them.

"Is that so?" Charlie asked, looking at the two men. "Why don't I see you walking away?" He didn't really expect them to answer. He crossed his arms over his chest.

"Because they're dumb as a stack of bricks," Eva said scornfully. Her voice trembled just a tiny bit, sending Charlie's protective instincts into overdrive.

"They're leaving now," he said, stepping forward. He was angry, and he was sure it showed, because neither Eva's uncle nor his friend would meet his gaze.

The two men backed up a few steps. "I don't know who the hell you are, but you're butting in on family business," Albert said angrily. He tried to act as if

Charlie's size wasn't at all intimidating, but Charlie noticed the man didn't exactly get up close to him.

Charlie smiled, baring his teeth. "Leave. Now. While you can still walk."

"Just go, Albert. And take your friend with you," Eva said, stepping in front of Charlie. "I don't want you here."

Charlie could tell she didn't want him to resort to violence, but he could see the small tremors she struggled to hide. *If I have to drag these two out of here by their feet, so be it,* he thought as he put a hand on her shoulder. Eva moved closer to him again, glaring at the two men. The one she'd called her uncle glared right back, and the idiot even took a step forward.

"Your mother would hate the way you're acting, Evangeline," Albert said. "Like a little baby."

Huh. Guess he found his balls, after all, Charlie thought as his anger slid into rage. "If you're not gone in thirty seconds, I'm going to pound you flat," he told the two men. He almost hoped they'd push it. His fists itched to take them apart. How dare they bother Eva? He didn't give a shit if the man was a relative. In fact, that made it a thousand times worse. *Talk about a sorry excuse for a man,* Charlie thought darkly. "I'll enjoy twisting your little dick right off if I have to, you know."

"Oh, the faggot talks big," Albert sneered.

"Oh my God, Albert, will you just *go* already? Do you have a death wish?" Eva sounded exasperated. Her voice had lost the tremor. "I told you I don't need help, and I certainly don't need you and your friend Bob getting all up in my business. You disgust me."

Charlie glared at Albert. "Do you think I don't mean it?" He flexed his fingers. He didn't often use his height and build to threaten other men, but he'd never finished a fight on the losing side. He was big, and he knew how to be an intimidating motherfucker. In this case, he'd enjoy putting his size to good use. Eva put her hand on his back. Instead of soothing him, it made him want to hit Albert harder. This little pervert and his friend were harassing Eva, and that made him want to break something, preferably their bones. Eva didn't deserve this shit.

"Fuck you. There's two of us, and only one of you," Bob said, clearly lacking in the brains department. "And I don't see you actually doing anything. You're just spouting threats."

"Okay, that does it," Charlie muttered. The idiot completely discounted Eva's ability to take care of herself, and that really irritated him. He stepped forward. Eva's hand slipped away as he moved, and the younger man scurried back, almost tripping, but Eva's uncle stood up to him. *Good. It'll be more fun this way*, he thought darkly.

"Who the hell do you think you are?" Albert asked belligerently. He faced off with Charlie as if the height difference meant nothing, the dumbass. "Eva is my niece. I have every right to be here."

This is going to be almost too easy, Charlie thought. He was happy to finally have a useful way of pounding out his lingering frustration. "After Eva told you to go? No, you do *not* have every right to be here." He reached out and grabbed the man by the front of the shirt, then hoisted him up onto his toes. "You don't get to harass Eva." he bit off through clenched teeth. "You don't even get to talk to her, you little shithead. I don't want to ever see you bother her again."

"You and what army?" Albert retorted.

"Oh my God, Albert," Eva said, clearly exasperated. "You're such an idiot." She glared at her uncle.

To Charlie's everlasting satisfaction, the man actually flinched when he saw the expression on her face, but his friend wasn't as perceptive.

"Who the fuck do you think you are?" Bob asked again, the little asshole.

"I'm Eva's boyfriend," Charlie growled at him. "And while I prefer not to do two things at once, I can certainly punch you out while choking the air out of this excuse for a man." He shook Albert like a wet rag, then twisted the fabric in his hands so that it cut off the asshole's airway. "And I won't even break a sweat doing it, so don't tempt me." He let go of Albert all at once, and the man fell to the ground, gasping and choking.

Eva stared at him for a moment, hands on her throat, and for a moment, Charlie thought she was about to kick him, but then she looked up at Charlie. "Boyfriend?" she mouthed at him, eyebrows lifted.

Charlie scowled at her, then turned his attention to the younger man. "Get. Out."

Bob had been watching Albert cough, frowning, but when Charlie spoke, he blanched, and then started backing away.

Eva's uncle heaved himself to his feet. "You won't get away with this," he said, voice raspy. He coughed again. His face was a particularly unattractive shade of red.

"Watch me." Charlie hoped he'd bruised the man's larynx. He hoped every time the man drew a breath it hurt like hell. "And if you think you can report this to the cops, think again. I have friends everywhere."

Albert glared, but he'd already started backing away. He grabbed Bob by the arm and dragged the man with him.

"And don't come back," Eva called, hands on her hips.

HOW LONG IS FOREVER?

Charlie stared at them until they slunk out of the yard, then looked at Eva. "Are you sure you're okay?" He reached out and tucked a stray curl behind her ear. He wanted to smooth his palm down all that dewy skin, but she looked like she was on her last nerve. *She might just break my finger if I try and touch her right now*, he thought, half amused, and half still worried about her.

"I ... what the hell, Charlie?" Eva finally asked, frowning up at him. "Boyfriend? Since when are you my boyfriend? Last I remember, you ran out of here like your pants were on fire."

Charlie flushed. He hadn't been thinking straight. Hell, he hadn't been thinking at *all*. And now that *that* particular word was spoken, he was going to have a hell of a time taking it back.

Mostly because I really don't want to take it back. She may be too young for me, but I can't stop what I feel. I can't stop wanting her, he thought, looking at Eva's flushed skin and unruly hair. She stared right back at him, bold and proud. He didn't want to hurt her. He didn't want to stay away from her. He didn't want to pretend anymore that he didn't want to fuck her long and sweet and hard in that pink-sheeted bed of hers, until they both collapsed.

Shit, he thought, as his heart suddenly lurched against his ribcage. *I could fall in love with this woman.*

Chapter Six

Eva stared at Charlie, wondering if her heart was strong enough to take this bullshit. "Boyfriend? Since when are you my boyfriend? Last I remember, you ran out of here like your pants were on fire," she said, instead of answering his question. Because really, she *wasn't* okay. She'd been trying to relax with a book and some sun, and instead her idiot Uncle Albert had shown up out of the blue. She hadn't seen him in years. She'd always disliked him, and after he'd skipped her mother's funeral, she'd relegated him to the group of people she had no intention of interacting with, family or not. She'd never understood why her mother put up with him, although she supposed it was hard to stop loving a little brother, even after he grew up into a jerk. And then the asshole had hit on her, with his disgusting friend, and she'd suddenly realized that for all her height, she really wasn't prepared to fight off two grown men all by herself.

And then Charlie had shown up like an avenging angel.

"Charlie? What exactly did you mean by that?" Eva pressed her fingers into his chest. He was looking at her as though she'd grown another head. What the hell *was* it with men? They were either full speed ahead or sudden stop, and she was damned tired of it.

"I'm sorry," Charlie said.

Eva rolled her eyes. *This* again. "Come on, Charlie. Give me a break. I'm in no mood." She wasn't sure if she wanted to kiss him for scaring the shit out of Albert and his friend and saving her from a full-scale assault, or yell at him for being such a jerk last Friday. She'd been depressed all weekend because of him. He'd given her the most amazing kiss of her life, and then he'd walked away as if it meant nothing. As if *she* meant nothing. And now he pulled this crazy declaration out of his ass, and every cell in her body celebrated the words as if he hadn't just broken her to pieces a few days ago. *I'm so totally losing it,* she thought, wishing she had the courage to walk away from him. Her fear of another rejection warred with her desperate need to ground herself in his warmth.

Charlie frowned down at her. "I couldn't let him get away with treating you like that," he said, as if that were any sort of answer to what she wanted to know.

Eva rolled her eyes *again*—at this rate she was going to have a first-rate headache in a few minutes—and stepped back. "Why are you here, Charlie?" she asked tiredly. She should have known he would avoid explaining himself. He might be a good person, but he was still a *guy*.

He glanced at her house, gaze flicking to her gutters, then back at her.

"No." Eva narrowed her eyes. "Do *not* tell me you're here to clean my fucking gutters." She rarely cursed, and never in front of Charlie, but this occasion felt like the right time to bust out her inner warrior. She didn't want to hear this from him. She didn't want to see him up on another ladder. He was the one who'd made her cry herself to sleep two nights in a row and eat ice cream for dinner, and now he was here to clean her roof as if none of that had happened.

He broke my heart. I don't know how that's possible, but he did it. And even as she had those thoughts, she looked at him, and he looked so fucking beautiful and strong that she wanted to throw herself into his arms and forget about all the crap in her life. He was big enough to hold her. He was the only man who'd *ever* been big enough to hold her. *But he said no,* she reminded herself. *He said no. Have some dignity, girl.*

Charlie stepped forward. "I can't do this anymore," he muttered, looking as desperate as she felt.

Eva stared at him. She wasn't going to give an inch until he met her halfway. "You're not doing anything, Charlie. That's the *problem*." Her voice cracked. Somehow, all the adrenaline from her encounter with Albert and his friend had transmuted into desire for Charlie. Eva knew letting go of him was the right thing to do, but how could she when he stood there in his old jeans and tight t-shirt, looking like every girl's dream come true? The silver at the edges of his dark hair made her want to run her fingers through it and muss it up. His light brown eyes made her want to close hers. And the intensity of his expression made her want to grab onto him and never, ever let go.

He reached out and tucked a stray curl behind her ear, fingers light and warm. "I can't pretend, Eva." His low voice sent curls of heat down her spine.

"Pretend what?" she asked, angrier now than when Albert had been bothering her. Getting him to talk was as hard as pulling teeth. Albert meant nothing to her. Charlie, unfortunately, meant everything. She had a sinking feeling that she'd been fooling herself for years. She'd never had a little girl's crush on him. She'd fallen in love, sometime back in her teen years, and hadn't quite realized it. *And isn't that a kick in the ass? I have to be the only woman who's ever fallen in love and not known it. Self-denial, thy name is Eva.* She bit the inside of her cheek, reaching for calm. It didn't work.

Charlie sighed. "I can't pretend that I don't feel anything for you, because I do." He swallowed. "I'm just a man, Eva. I'm not made of stone."

Do I push a little more? Do I step back? Eva pursed her lips, then made her decision. "You're going to have to give me a little more than that, Charlie."

HOW LONG IS FOREVER?

To her surprise, he cupped her cheeks in his warm palms. "I want you so much I can't sleep. I think about Friday's kiss when I should be working. I dream about you when I should be awake." He shook his head. "And I feel so damned guilty about it. You're too young for me. You're my friend's daughter. I shouldn't be thinking of you this way." He sighed, but he didn't let go. His work-roughened hands steadied her face, tilting her up as if he were about to kiss her. His gaze flicked down to her lips.

Eva flushed as a rush of need swept through her. *God*, she wanted him to kiss her. She swayed closer, until she could feel the heat rising from his skin. "But you do. You *do* feel that way about me," she told him, trying one last time to make him *see*. "This isn't just on me, Charlie." She lifted her hands and touched his wrists. Was it her imagination, or did he tremble? For the first time in days she didn't regret propositioning him. Maybe she'd had to ask him in order to wake him up. Maybe all her misery would be worth it.

"You're right. I *do* feel that way," Charlie repeated, thumb brushing over her lower lip. "When my brother Frankie was dying, I promised him that I would make sure your dad would be okay. They were best friends. And then after he died, Phil took care of *me*, instead. I never expected him to step into my older brother's shoes, but somehow, he did. Your dad was a special person." He inhaled and let out the breath slowly. "And that's why I feel so damned guilty for wanting you. He's not here to punch me for it."

"My dad would never punish you for caring about me," Eva said, tears pricking her eyes. "He would probably be thrilled if we got together. He always told me that when love happened, you had to hold on tight with both hands. He was a good man." She gathered her courage. Charlie had to know what she felt to be true. "He would be happy to see us together. He wouldn't be angry."

Charlie shook his head. "I don't know—"

Eva cut him off. "I *do* know."

Charlie looked at her for a moment. "You're so sure. I envy that."

Eva rolled her eyes. "He was my dad," she said simply. "He was a good person."

Charlie tried to move his hands, but Eva wouldn't let him.

"No." She looked at him, willing him to understand.

He let her hold his hands while he held her gaze. "When his wound went septic, I promised him I'd take care of you and your mom." His expression darkened. "And that means making sure you're okay. It means making sure you're safe and that you have everything you need. It doesn't mean stripping off your clothes and kissing every single inch of your body." He shook his head. "I'm a selfish bastard for wanting you so bad."

God, when he says stuff like that, I feel like I'm going to explode, Eva thought, swallowing hard. "You're not selfish, because you *did* take care of us," she made herself say. She remembered how he'd been there for her and her mom. He'd held her mom when she cried. And then he'd held Eva when her mom had died. She'd been a mess, and he hadn't once flinched. How could she not have a crush on this man? She licked her lips, smiling when she heard his soft groan.

"I can't stop thinking of how perfectly you fit me, Eva." Charlie's voice had dipped down in its lower register, and the rumbly tone did crazy thing to her insides. Eva inhaled, struggling for calm. She noticed that he didn't try to step back again. He didn't take his hands away from her face. She watched him close his eyes as if his head hurt.

"It's okay, Charlie. You're allowed to have feelings. Did it ever occur to you that maybe we're supposed to be together? That maybe all the shit we've been through means we're allowed to enjoy each other? Because what is the point of life, otherwise?" Eva reached up and touched his cheek. "You can have this. You can have *me*."

"It feels wrong to want you," Charlie said quietly.

"But you do anyway," Eva said again.

"Yes," he agreed, opening his eyes. "God help me."

"God isn't here. I am." Eva put her hands on his wrists. "It's not wrong, Charlie." She tilted her head, trying a different tack. "How old are you?" She fingered the silver at his temples. She liked his maturity. She liked that he wasn't some callow teen.

"Thirty-five," he said.

Not that old, she thought. "You're only fourteen years older than me." Eva smiled at him. "You idiot." Charlie tried to step back, but she hung onto him, forcing him to stay. "You're making a mountain out of a molehill."

"I'm fourteen years too old for you," he insisted.

"You realize that you're not even old enough to be my father? You're ten years younger than my dad was, Charlie." Eva very deliberately took a step forward, knowing as she did that she could very well be setting herself up for another rejection. It would kill her, but she couldn't seem to stop the hope that she felt when she looked at him. "You're a big jerk," she whispered, drawing his head down to her. "I don't want to go through my whole life without making love with you, Charlie." She flushed at her bold words. She didn't think she'd ever said "making love" out loud before, but the look in his eyes as she said it made the embarrassment worth it. "I don't want to be alone anymore." She touched her lips to his.

He groaned. "Eva," he whispered against her mouth. "Fuck." Then he kissed her, and it felt as if the world turned itself upside down.

Eva clung to him as he dragged her up against his body. He was everything that was good and right in her life, and she'd be damned if she'd let him run away from her again. She slid her hands into his hair and growled, "You're mine, Charlie. I might not know what the hell I'm doing, but I know that *this*—" She emphasized her words with a tug of his hair. "—doesn't happen often. And when it does, you have to grab on with both hands and hang on. My mother told me that. She learned it the hard way, so I believe her. My grandpa was an asshole for leaving her and my grandma the way he did, but Mom said it taught her to recognize real love when it happened. When she met my dad, she knew he was the real deal. He was everything her own dad wasn't." She kissed Charlie, lingering over the softness of his lips. "The difference in our ages doesn't matter when it feels like this." He looked at her steadily, and Eva almost lost her courage, but she refused to back down now. "I don't want a lesson anymore. I want it all." She took a deep breath. "I want everything. I want you."

"This thing between us?" Charlie murmured, kissing the corner of her mouth. "This is fire, Eva sweet. This is crazy. You should be running the other direction, not holding onto me. I'm too old for you. I feel like a fucking perv, robbing the cradle, and I still can't stop." He rubbed his stubble-roughened cheek against hers as his hands roamed her body. His palms settled on her ass and hauled her up against him.

Eva gasped. His cock pressed into her hip. She writhed, trying to get closer.

"God," he burst out, breathing faster as she clutched at him. "I don't want to hurt you." He let her slide down his body.

Eva swayed into him, still drunk on his heat. "You're not going to hurt me. No man so wary of letting himself feel something, *anything,* could ever hurt me. And if you do?" She shrugged. "So what? What's the worst that could happen?" she asked, knowing even as she said the words that she'd be devastated if he walked away. *But I don't care*, she thought recklessly, grabbing onto this opportunity with both hands.

"Sweetheart," he whispered. "You don't know what you're asking for."

"You're worth the risk to me, Charlie," Eva replied. She boldly wound a leg around his calf. "Am I worth the risk to you? Are you willing to stop being afraid?" She leaned back so she could look into his face. *He's second guessing himself,* she thought hopefully, reading the uncertainty in his expression. *Good. I want him off balance. Right?*

Charlie frowned. "Fear is relative."

Eva huffed. "I'm not sure I could forgive you if you say no again, Charlie. Sure, I'll survive, because I have at least a little self-respect, but I won't be able to see you for a long time without crying."

"Eva—"

She cut him off. "You realize that, right? You won't be able to just come back and pretend that it never happened. I'm willing to try, Charlie, but there are consequences if you walk away." She thought of her miserable weekend. If he left her again, it would be a thousand times worse. She knew some people would say that she was moving things too fast, but she firmly believed that when you knew, you knew. *And I've known Charlie was the one for me for years now*, she reminded herself.

He leaned his forehead on hers. "I'm out of my comfort zone here. I don't know what I'm doing. I'm afraid your dad wouldn't approve of this."

"You know my father wasn't like that. He would be happy we found each other." Eva frowned at him. "You'll hurt me more if you walk away from me again, Charlie. Think about that." Her frustration with him gave her strength. If he didn't give in soon, she was going to smack him.

Charlie slid his arms around her and held her tight. "If we do this, it's not going to be a one-time thing. I can't do a hookup with you, Eva." He rolled his hips.

God, she thought as her heart pounded. His body felt hard as hell and twice as hot. *He thinks that's a bad thing?* Eva shuddered. "You told my uncle you were my boyfriend. What if he didn't believe you? What if he comes back?" she asked him, playing her last card. If jealousy didn't work, then she didn't know what would.

Charlie growled and swept her up into his arms. "That's it. That just pushed me over the edge."

Eva gasped, clutching at his shoulders. "Charlie! Are you crazy?" What if he dropped her? She wasn't some tiny little model. Her face burned as she thought of all the ice cream she'd stuffed herself with the past few days. "I'm too heavy."

He ignored her protests as he strode up to the deck. "Don't be ridiculous. In case you haven't noticed, I'm twice your size, Eva. You're not fat. You're not too tall, and you're not too heavy for me. Except for being an infant, you're perfect," he said, almost biting out the words.

"I'm not an infant, I'm a grown woman," Eva

protested breathlessly.

"You're a gorgeous infant, and I can't seem to keep my hands off of you," Charlie said. "If your idiot uncle comes back looking for trouble, he'll find me here, ready to smash his face in. I'm almost hoping he does come back. It'll give me something to vent my frustration on." He headed towards the back door of the house. "And what the hell is this scrap of nothing that you're wearing?" He flicked a thumb over her halter strap.

Eva bit her lip as she flushed. In his arms, she felt tiny, despite the fact that she *knew* she was anything but small. "It's an old halter. It's comfy." And it suddenly felt way too small. Her nipples pebbled into hard points against the soft cloth, and she knew he could see them.

"It's making me crazy," he said, kicking open the back door. "It barely covers you. I can see your nipples." He swept through the kitchen to the hall, and then to her room. "I want to tear it off with my fucking *teeth*." He tossed her on her bed.

Oh, my God. This is Charlie unleashed? This is even better than I'd hoped. Eva landed on her back, skin tingling. *He wants to rip my clothes off. Yay,* she thought, trying on the idea for size. She found that she liked it. She liked it very much. She eyed him as he stood over her, all wild eyes and disheveled hair. If this old halter did that to him, she'd definitely have to buy more. *Maybe in a smaller size*, she thought, grinning at him. "I don't think gnawing through fabric is good for your teeth," she said, just to tease a rise out of him.

He didn't disappoint her. "Fuck my teeth, Eva," he said, coming down on top of her. He straddled her body, trapping her legs, then ran his fingertips along her shoulders and down her arms as she squirmed. "This is your last chance."

Oh, good. Eva licked her lips. "Last chance for what?"

"To think about what you're asking. Once I make love to you, nothing will ever be the same between us," Charlie said, voice dropping again into his low register. "*You* won't be the same. I'll be your first man, no matter what happens between us in the future."

Eva shivered. *Is that a threat? If so, it failed. Miserably.* She looked up at him. The bulge in his jeans was intimidating, but the look in his eyes was everything she'd ever wanted: heat and love and need all wrapped up into one. He thought he couldn't care for her the right way, but his feelings were there on his face, and she'd known him long enough to read him.

"Charlie," she said, feeling like there wasn't enough air in the room. Hell, there wasn't enough air on the *planet*. "I've wanted you since I was fourteen. I'm not going to change my mind now." She looked away, suddenly uncertain. Years of being called too fat and too tall weren't so easy to dismiss, after all. She bit her lip. "But no one has ever wanted *me*. I understand if you truly aren't attracted to me. I don't want to push you into it." She squeezed her eyes shut, mentally kicking herself. Why hadn't she considered that before she all but threw herself at him? Again?

"Eva, Jesus. For the last time, you're not fat. You're not too tall. You're fucking perfect, and those other boys don't have a clue what to do with you, because they are *boys*," Charlie said, a hint of anger in his voice. "I'm not. I'm a grown man, and I know what the hell I'm doing." He shook her gently. "Do I look like I don't want you? Open your eyes and look at me."

Her eyes flew open. He was undoing his jeans. *Oh my God,* she thought, breathless all over again. She couldn't tear her gaze away from his fingers.

HOW LONG IS FOREVER?

"This is me desperate to have you, Eva," Charlie said. He'd got the zipper down, and he cupped his erection where it bulged out against the soft fabric of his underwear. "I jacked off at home an hour ago, because I knew I'd be coming here, and I knew the moment I saw you I'd be like this." He wrapped a hand around his cock. Pre-cum wet a spot on the fabric. "It didn't help me one bit." He stroked himself through his boxers. "This is what you do to me. This is how crazy you make me."

Eva's mouth went dry. She'd never heard a man talk like this. She'd never heard *Charlie* talk like this. She had no idea what to do with her hands. "Oh." Her face burned as she thought about him masturbating to thoughts of her. *Talk about a head rush.*

He smiled, slow and sure, and Eva could tell he'd finally committed to giving into this thing between them. "I'm hard for you. I want to put my cock in your pussy, Eva. I want to fuck you until we both forget how to speak. Do you still think I give a shit how heavy you think you are? How tall you are?" He took off his shirt and tossed it aside, muscles flexing. "You're fucking perfect for me. All my life I've been too big. Women like big guys only until the clothes come off, and then they freak out."

Eva's gaze landed on the thick muscles of his chest. "I'm not freaking out," she whispered. If she was perfect for him, he was perfect for her. Somehow, she'd always known it would be like this. *Is this why I sucked at dating? Maybe I've been waiting for Charlie all along.*

"I know." Charlie's grin told her he knew exactly what she was feeling, and it was as far from freaking out as the moon was from the sun.

Eva lifted her hands and ran her fingers through the sprinkling of hair along his pectorals. She lingered over his tattoo, the small bird in flight just at the tip of her finger. She'd always loved his ink, and now that she got to see it up close… *I thought I was aroused before, but I had no idea,* she thought, mind racing in a thousand directions. She wanted to touch him, and she wanted him to touch her, and she didn't know if those two things were simultaneously possible. She couldn't forget that her very first kiss had been with Charlie only a few days ago. Now, he was half naked. What the hell did she know about pleasing a man?

"You ready?" Charlie asked.

"I've been ready," Eva told him boldly, pushing aside her doubts.

Charlie leaned down, kissing her lightly, and then bit her lower lip until it stung. "No turning back now," he murmured, hands on her hips. "God, you feel good." He stretched out over her, heavy and solid.

Eva writhed beneath him. She loved the weight of him. For the first time in her life, she felt petite. "More. Please, Charlie."

"More? You'll get more." Charlie slid a hand under her halter top and tweaked her nipple. "God, this halter is tiny." He leaned back up and took the fabric in both hands. "I hope you don't mind if I tear it off of you."

Before Eva could say a word, he clenched his muscles and tore the fabric in two. Heat shot through her as her breasts spilled loose. "Oh my God," she gasped.

Charlie smiled. "Do you trust me?"

Eva stared at him. She did. Of course she did. She trusted him with her life. Now she was trusting him with her heart. "I do."

Charlie's eyes flared dark. "Then let me make you feel everything."

Chapter Seven

Charlie trailed his fingers down her beautiful, silky skin, wondering what the hell he thought he was doing. He'd stepped over the line, and then instead of venturing forward cautiously, he'd obliterated the trail and pushed his way deep into the wilds. Eva stared up at him with wide, innocent eyes, and he could barely keep his hands from trembling. He tried to remind himself that this was her first time, but the thought only made him crazier. He squeezed his cock until it hurt. And then he squeezed her, desperate to sink into her soft heat.

"I'm going to love you until you can't think, sweetheart. Until you can't breathe," he said, cupping her pert, young breasts.

She sucked in a shocked gasp when he rolled her delicious little nipples between his fingers. He didn't pinch them … yet. He was saving that for later, for when his cock was so deep inside her she could taste his hunger. "Beautiful," he breathed, smoothing his palms down her torso to her waist. Eva was so tiny compared to him—he couldn't believe she thought she was too big. She wasn't skinny, thank God, and she had muscle under that gorgeous, sweet skin, so as far as he was concerned, she was literally the perfect woman for him. For the first time in his life, he didn't feel like he was going to break the woman in bed with him.

"Don't stop," she said, voice soft. Bashful.

Charlie smiled at her as he deliberately tucked his fingers into the waistband of her shorts. "I know what you want," he said, letting his voice drop into its lower register.

Eva shivered.

Charlie slid his fingers in further, swallowing at the heat rising from her skin. His cock ached, but he held himself ruthlessly in check. She asked him to show her what sex was like, and he'd be damned if he'd rut into her like some idiot boy. She was going to beg him for it. He needed her to feel just as insane as he did. He couldn't deny his need for her anymore, as uncomfortable as he was with it. He was a grown man, and she was barely a woman, and fuck him if that didn't make him want her even more.

"These are in the way," he said, undoing the button and sliding down the zipper. He pushed his guilt aside as her belly quivered under his touch. "Can I take them off?"

"Of course," Eva said, but had to stop and clear her throat to continue. "Yes."

Here we go. Charlie drew her shorts off her body, closing his eyes as the sweet, musky smell of her arousal hit his nose. She was so wet her panties were damp. He slid down the bed and nuzzled into her groin, inhaling deeply. Fuck, she was so freaking perfect for him. He gripped her hips with his fingers as he fought with his libido. Self-control won, but only barely.

"Oh my God, what are you doing? Charlie?" Eva tried to push him away, but he caught her wrists, holding her gently but firmly.

"I'll stop if you want me to," he said, voice fucking shaking, damn it to hell. "I don't want to hurt you."

"I was just lying out in the sun. I'm all sweaty and stinky," she protested, trying to squirm away. All she succeeded in doing was wrapping her legs around his shoulders.

And that's precisely where I want them, Charlie thought, nuzzling her mound again. "That explains why you smell so fucking good," he said, looking at the outline of her clit pressing against her underwear. He took a deep breath and then blew it out against the fabric, heating her up even more. "I want to eat you up."

Eva cried out as the warmth of his breath hit her sensitive skin.

"Do you want me to stop?" he asked, breathing on her again and then again. He was going to give her an orgasm with his mouth, and then he was going to give her another with his cock, and maybe a third with his fingers. "If you want me to stop, all you have to do is say the word." He prayed she didn't, but this was all new to her. He'd understand if she backed down. He wouldn't exactly *enjoy* it, not with the state his body was in, but he'd understand. "Eva?"

She shook her head as her legs tightened around his shoulders.

"Words, Eva. I need words. I won't do anything you don't want me to do, but you have to say yes before I go ahead," Charlie told her. He wanted her to feel in control. He wanted her to choose everything he wanted to do to her. He rolled his erection into the mattress, trying to get some relief. He'd never felt so wild in bed before.

"Please," Eva whispered, hands fisted in her comforter. Her curly hair lay in wild disarray along the comforter. Her cheeks flushed pink beneath tightly closed eyes.

"Please, what?" Charlie asked softly, thumbs gently circling just outside her labia. The sound of her voice did crazy things to his heart. The scent of her body did crazy things to his cock. "Talk to me, sweetheart."

"Please, don't stop," Eva said, breathless.

Charlie smiled. "I'm going to lick your clit until you orgasm, and then I'm going to feed my cock into you nice and slow until you feel so full you can't move," he said roughly, enjoying her little moans. He liked the way she reacted when he used explicit words. "Can I take these off?" He tucked his fingers under the elastic of her panties. He looked up the line of her body, enjoying her curves.

She nodded.

"Say please," he told her. "Say it out loud."

"Oh, fuck," she panted as he moved his fingers beneath the thin elastic.

"Words, Eva," Charlie reminded her, gritting his teeth. She smelled like fucking heaven. He couldn't wait to put his mouth on her. Cream seeped from her sweet cunny, slicking his fingers, and he hadn't even gotten her completely naked yet.

"You can take them off," she finally said, sounding like he'd wrung her out.

Charlie snapped the elastic with a quick jerk, and then grinned at her shocked gasp. "I'll buy you new ones," he promised her. "I'll buy you a thousand new pairs of panties." And then without further ado, he licked her from her ass to her clit. Eva bucked, and he wound his arms around her thighs to keep her in place. "Hang on, honey," he said roughly. He waited until she'd wound her fingers into his hair, and then he settled down to play with her sweet bud until she exploded. He licked the tip of her clit, then gently closed his teeth on the hood and moved back and forth until her back bowed off the bed. "You like?" he asked, sliding his thumbs along her labia. She was nice and pink and slippery. She kept her hair trimmed short but not shaved, not that it mattered to him. He liked a woman with hair down there. "Eva?" He looked up to see her face, but her head was thrown back. "Talk to me, baby."

"Yes, oh my God, don't fucking stop now, Charlie," she said, voice desperate.

Perfect. He smiled again and settled back down.

"I'm going to put my fingers in you. I don't want to hurt you, Eva, but it might feel tight." He waited for her nod, and then he slowly eased one finger inside. "Okay?" He reminded himself that this was her first time. He had to be patient. He had to take his time. *Torture, when all I want to do is ram myself into her sweet heat.*

"Yes," she gasped, hips rising and trying to get him deeper. "It's good, Charlie. So good."

Charlie licked her clit a few times, keeping her right on the edge. When he backed off, she protested, but he eased another finger inside. She was so tight, and so fucking sweet. He didn't know how he was going to get his cock in there, but he'd manage. Somehow. He gritted his teeth, trying not to come all over her bed like a horny thirteen-year-old.

"Feels so good," Eva said, hands tightening in his hair now. She tugged, trying to get him to move his mouth back up to her clit. He obliged, sliding his fingers in and out. He sucked her bud back into his mouth, flicking it with his tongue while he slid another finger into her cunny. She writhed, moaning, and he grabbed her ass with his free hand, lifting her to his mouth. She cried out.

And she worries about being too big? he thought, confused all over again by her insecurity. Eva's ass was the perfect size to fill his hand, and she was sturdy enough that he didn't have to worry about hurting her. He sucked her faster, fucking her with his fingers. She shivered, head thrashing as she squeezed his head with her thighs, and Charlie settled in to make her absolutely insane.

****

Eva couldn't see, couldn't speak... Hell, she could barely breathe. Charlie kept her right on the edge of orgasm with his mouth and fingers, expertly teasing and sucking until she thought she was going to lose her freaking mind. At first, she worried that she was going to hurt him—she wasn't small, and she didn't want to crush his face, but he didn't even seem to notice her thighs closing around his shoulders. After a while, as he kept tormenting her, she forgot about her belly and her stupid, too long legs, and let go completely. Any man strong enough to go down on her right after she'd been sweating buckets in the sun was a man strong enough to deal with her thighs strangling him, or so she told herself. Frankly, she could hardly believe this was actually happening. She'd *never* expected him to give her oral—not in her wildest dreams. She'd mostly hoped for a kiss and maybe a pleasant bout of first-time sex that didn't hurt too much. Instead, she got Charlie going wild on her. *Girl, you sure know how to pick 'em.*

"Eva, you taste so fucking sweet," he said, coming up for air. He fucked her slow and easy with his fingers. "I could eat you out all damned day."

And I'd let you, Eva though, trying to get his mouth back where she wanted it. She remembered how embarrassed she'd been when he'd first ripped off her panties, but now, all she wanted was more. More of his mouth, more of his fingers. More of *him.* For a moment, she frantically tried to remember the last time she'd shaved down there, and of course, it had been a thousand years ago, but he didn't seem to care. She wasn't bare, and she wasn't perfectly squeaky clean, and yet he'd dived in anyway. *I thought guys were supposed to be grossed out by this?* she mused.

"I'm going to eat you again after I put my cock in you. You'll be all soft and sensitive, baby. I want to taste my cum in your cunny," Charlie murmured, fingers moving lazily, and Eva realized that her decision to proposition him was certainly the right one. He seemed to get off on giving her pleasure, and what twenty-year-old guy would do that? Hell, they wouldn't even go on a date with her.

Their loss, she thought, squirming as Charlie teased her but didn't let her fall over the edge. His dirty talk had her face flaming, but she didn't care. If anything, it revved her up higher.

"You'll be dying for another orgasm," Charlie said, kissing the sensitive spot where her thigh met her mound.

"I'm dying for one now," she gasped, hooking her ankles together. "Please, Charlie." She tried to yank his face back where she wanted it, but she couldn't budge him. *Damn, he's strong.*

"Patience," he said, smiling against her leg. He finger-fucked her slow and easy.

Older men are definitely the way to go, Eva thought, still clutching his hair. He didn't sound unsure anymore. He didn't sound as though he regretted making love to her, and deep inside, Eva slowly let herself begin to hope that this thing between them just might work out in the long run.

"You ready, sweetheart?" Charlie finally asked her, interrupting the haze of pleasure spiraling through her brain.

She nodded, not trusting herself to speak.

"Tell me what you want, Eva," he said, leisurely fucking her with his thumbs. The callouses on his fingers were just enough to add texture without pain. She loved that he was a man who used his hands. She loved that he was using them on *her*. "Come on, baby. Tell me what you want."

Eva flushed, hating that he was making her say the words. "I want you to let me c-come," she managed, stuttering on the last word.

"You want my cock inside you before or after you orgasm?" Charlie asked, giving her a choice she could barely comprehend.

Eva looked down at him. His mouth was slick with her cream, and he still had his fingers inside her body. "I don't know," she said, voice trembling, wishing he would just lick her again so she didn't have to think.

"If you wait for me to be inside you when you come, it might be easier for your first time because a little bit of pain makes it all the sweeter," Charlie said, sliding his fingers in and out of her pussy. "And you're so fucking tight, baby. It might be a very, very tight fit." He smiled a bit sheepishly. "I'm not a small man."

No, you are not, Eva thought biting her lip. She wasn't sure how many fingers he was using, but there were enough to make the stretch almost, but not quite, uncomfortable. "Okay," she said, making her decision. "I'll wait for my orgasm," she added before he could prompt her to be more specific. Saying those words aloud felt weird, but then, this whole situation was weird, wasn't it? *Sex is weird,* she thought, wondering how the hell she ended up here, with Charlie. *Oh, that's right. You pursued him relentlessly and without shame*, she reminded herself.

Charlie grinned up at her, looking suddenly younger than she'd ever seen him. "You won't regret it, sweetheart." He eased his fingers out and then stood up to take off his jeans.

Eva already knew she wouldn't regret it. Even if it hurt. *Even if he leaves me after it's all over, I won't regret this,* she vowed. Charlie was the only man she'd ever really wanted, and he was here with her, right now. In her bed, making love to her. He'd had his fingers in her pussy. He'd had his *mouth* on her *clit*. She flushed as she watched him strip his pants off, and then his boxers.

Oh my God, she thought, mesmerized. This was her very first, real life, close up view of a grown man's aroused body, and Charlie was a hell of a lot of man. His cock jutted out from his body, thick and rosy, while his balls hung below. He looked a lot bigger than she'd expected. A *lot* bigger. *How the hell is that going to fit?* she wondered, biting her lip. A drop of pre-cum slid from the slit on the crown while she stared at him. Eva reached out instinctively, wanting to feel his heat on her fingertips, but he moved away before she could touch him.

"Oh no, baby. If you touch me now, I won't be able to keep from coming all over your beautiful fingers," Charlie said, climbing back on the bed. His cock bobbed as he moved.

Eva stared at it, wondering what he'd taste like.

"And if you keep looking at me like that, I'm going to lose it," Charlie said, voice raspy. He held a foil packet in his hand. He dropped it on the comforter and cupped her knees.

Eva blushed. She wasn't sure if he was serious, or just trying to compliment her, but either way, there was no denying that there was a whole lot of aroused male in her bed with her. She glanced down at the condom.

"I'm on the pill," she said, a little worried about speaking up. She wanted to feel him, skin to skin. She didn't want her first time to be with a condom, but she didn't know how he'd react to her wish. "I don't want to use a condom for my first time."

Charlie paused, gaze arrested. "I've never had sex without a condom. Ever." He glanced down at her breasts, then her pussy, and then he inhaled long and slow. "God, the thought of going bareback…" His voice trailed off as his gaze went back to her cunny.

Eva licked her lips. "Then you're sort of a virgin,

too."

Charlie looked up at her face, and then he laughed. "I guess I am." He tilted his head. "Are you sure about this?" He blew out a breath. "I feel like I should be giving you the safe sex talk." He shook his head. "Going bareback is a big deal."

Annoyed, Eva sat up and grabbed his wrists. "Don't you dare." The thought of him lecturing her in the middle of sex about condoms made her want to throw something. "I'm not a child, Charlie. I'm a grown woman. And you were just staring at my breasts so I know that you know this."

"True," Charlie said wryly, glancing at her boobs again. "Okay, honey. We'll do it without." He laughed. "You don't have to twist my arm." He slid his hands up past her elbows and before she knew what happened, he was on his back on her bed with her straddling him. His cock poked up hot and hard against her pussy, and she sucked in a breath, shocked at how silky he felt.

"What are you doing?" she asked, confused. She didn't know where to put her hands. She didn't know where to put *herself*. She knelt up awkwardly—it couldn't be comfortable for him being crushed like that, could it? "I'm too big for you."

Charlie rolled his eyes. "Eva, I could pick you up without breaking a sweat." He lifted her by her waist, demonstrating a truly unholy level of fitness.

Eva froze as she stared at the muscles in his arms bulging. *Damn. That's really,* really *impressive,* she thought, fighting the urge to squirm. She didn't want him to drop her.

"See?" he said, laughter in his voice as he held her in midair. His grip on her waist was firm, but rock steady. "Now, stop with the worrying. I'm a *lot* bigger than you are."

Eva squeaked when he slid her back down his bent knees and his cock nudged her clit. "Oh God," she said, looking down. The rosy head of his erection peeked out from between her mound like an obscene sex toy. Charlie rolled her, somehow, and he slid his shaft all along her slit in exactly the right way to make her crazy.

"There. Just like that," he said, voice thick. "Come on, sweetheart. Fuck me like you want to."

Eva shuddered, then tried moving. She lifted her hips, and then slid down. His shaft didn't go in the right place so she took him in hand, encouraged by his low gasp. She tucked him against her clit and rolled her hips, and then she couldn't help doing it again, and then again. His cock felt so freaking good down there.

"Mmm, yeah, baby. Just like that," he said, encouraging her with his hands and his body. "Ride me."

Eva trembled, holding onto his arms until her thighs grew tired. "I'm so close," she said, shimmying her hips. She couldn't stop squirming on him. He was big and hard and strong, but somehow, she needed *more*. "I don't know what I'm doing wrong." She bit her lip, trying to move faster. It didn't help.

"You're doing everything right, Eva," Charlie said, hands going to her hips. "You just need a bit more." He lifted her up, then flexed his body so that his cock slotted right up against her cunny. "It's just the right time for this," he said, angling her forward. He tilted his hips, and the next thing she knew, his cock was sliding between her labia.

"Oh," she gasped, shuddering as he breached her inner lips. "Charlie—"

"I've got you," he said, rolling his body so his cock slid in further. "You're in control here, Eva." He rolled a little more. "Remember all you have to do is kneel up and everything stops."

Eva dug her fingers into his shoulders. When her pussy started to feel pinched, she instinctively lifted up.

"See?" Charlie murmured, hands soothing down her waist to her ass. "Everything we do is in your hands."

Eva bit her lower lip, inching down again. She felt so full, but at the same time, too empty. "I need more," she said, swallowing hard against the pinch. Why did this have to be so difficult for women? It wasn't fair.

"Easy, baby. There's no rush." Charlie trailed his fingers up her belly to her breasts. He cupped them, then rolled her nipples. "God, these are gorgeous," he said, leaning up and sucking one into his mouth.

Eva moaned as he slid in further. She could hardly believe that Charlie could not only hold her up, but half-sit up on her bed while doing it, and make her crazy with pleasure at the same time. *He isn't kidding about being strong*, she thought hazily. He suckled her nipple, then moved to the other one as she rocked her hips, pushing his cock further and further inside her body. When her ass met his balls, she swallowed and dug her fingers into the solid mass of his shoulders. He felt hot and huge and impossibly big inside her. Her cunny ached, and she wasn't quite sure if it was actual pain, or if it just felt weird, or what.

"Is this right?" she whispered, squeezing her internal muscles experimentally. He felt even bigger when she did that. Charlie sucked in a breath and tipped his head back, pupils blown wide with his arousal. Eva trembled at the look on his face. He wasn't smiling.

"It's perfectly right, Eva," he croaked, visibly swallowing.

Eva tightened her internal muscles again, enjoying the way his face went taut. "Charlie. Help," she said, digging her fingers into his solid shoulders until his gaze met hers.

Charlie's eyes crackled as he looked at her. "Time to make love," he said, voice breaking as he slid his arms around her, slid out a bit, and then thrust up inside her again, hard.

Eva cried out as the base of his cock pressed right into her clit. The stretch of him burned all the way from the top of her head to her pussy. She'd never felt anything quite like this before, not even when she used her little vibrator. *Which in no way prepared me for this,* she thought, trembling. She clenched her inner muscles again, and Charlie huffed out a breath.

"God, Eva. Do that again," he commanded, sounding wrecked. His fingers flexed on her ass. "Feels so fucking good." He licked his lips. "You feel so fucking perfect, sweetheart."

Eva did it again, deciding that she liked the way he felt inside her. Given the way Charlie shuddered, he liked it, too. He thrust inside again. "Oh, fuck," she gasped, eyes closing. She held on as he did it again, and then again. Sparks of pleasure rocketed through her, combining with the ache in her core. *So, close,* she thought, and then her ability to hold herself up failed. Charlie caught her, mouth in a tight line as his hips rolled in perfect rhythm.

"I've got you," he growled, looking down between their bodies. "Jesus, that's a beautiful sight." He looked up again. "Hang on to me, Eva."

She wrapped her arms around his neck. "Please, Charlie," she begged, but she had no idea what the hell she was asking for. "Please."

Somehow, Charlie *did* know. He shifted his weight to make room and then slipped a hand between them to play with her clit. "Yeah, baby. Just like that," he said, still thrusting up. "You're so fucking hot like this, Eva."

She threw her head back as her body lifted. His legs felt like steel bands beneath her, and his grip around her waist almost hurt, but she didn't care. He slid a finger down to her core and then back up again to her clit. When he pinched her, she screamed. Waves of incandescent pleasure bowed her back, and Charlie grunted as she shattered. He tucked his face in her neck and jerked up hard, fucking her furiously. The motion somehow pushed more pleasure through her, and she dimly registered his hands on her ass, holding her tightly as he thrust. When he shuddered, gasping against her skin, warmth flooded her pussy.

Did he just come? she wondered, but he rolled his hips, and more pleasure slid through her, scattering her thoughts. She gasped, holding on for dear life until she could breathe again, a thousand and one years later. *What just happened?* she thought, groggy and too tired to lift her face. Charlie's shoulder was comfy, and he smelled divine, so she didn't even try to move until he sighed and kissed her temple.

"Are you okay?" he asked softly.

Okay is an understatement. Eva lifted her head and looked him right in the eyes. "Wow," she said, flushing. She felt like she'd just had an out of body experience. The thought that she'd finally lost her virginity, and to *Charlie* of all men, was too insane to believe, even though she was naked and in his arms. *And he's still inside you,* she reminded herself, struggling to wrap her mind around that fact. She'd pinch herself if Charlie wouldn't be sure to think she was nuts. "I just—" She tried to express her complete amazement, but then shook her head. "Wow."

Charlie laughed, eyes crinkling at the corners. His hair was a wreck, and Eva knew that was her fault. *Too bad.* She smoothed a hand along his dark locks, lingering on the sprinkling of grey at his temples. The silver just made him look even hotter. *He's a silver fox*, she thought fondly.

"Wow is a good way of putting it," he murmured, shifting them both. His softening erection slid out of her pussy, sending tingling aftershocks of pleasure through her body.

"Whoa," she said, biting her lip. That felt weird. He was still firm, but not quite as hard as he'd been just a moment ago. She looked down, blushing as she saw his cock glistening with their juices.

Charlie chuckled. "You sure you're okay?"

She nodded. "I think so." She tightened her muscles experimentally. She felt maybe a tiny bit sore?

"Mmm. Good." Charlie said, kissing her again.

Eva didn't know how he did it, but she ended up on the bed, tucked along his side. Her pussy tingled deliciously. *I could stay like this all day long,* she mused lazily, but then Charlie's softened cock brushed against her thigh. She bit her lip, wondering if he felt as strange as she did. She wished he could've stayed inside, maybe forever. She liked him there. She liked knowing she'd been the first woman he'd ever made love to without a condom. Her heart lurched as she realized he was looking at her, light brown eyes too clear for comfort.

"Are you sure you're okay?" he asked softly, tucking a stray curl behind her ear.

She nodded. "Of course."

"There's no 'of course' the first time," he said, cupping her cheek. "I didn't hurt you, did I?"

Eva wrinkled her brow at him. "No, of course not. You made sure of that." Her face went hot as she thought of all the things he'd done to her. She'd been so revved up, she wouldn't have cared if it *had* hurt. "It was amazing. *You* were amazing." She watched, fascinated, as *he* flushed, and then she giggled. "No one ever told you that before?"

"Contrary to what you think, I haven't had all that many partners," Charlie said ruefully, shaking his head. "And you may have just spoiled me forever. I've never had sex with anyone quite like you." He sounded surprised.

"I hope that's a good thing." Eva could hardly believe she was flirting with him. Now. After everything.

"You have to ask?" Charlie chuckled. "Yes, Eva. It's a good thing." He kissed her softly. "It's a very good thing."

"You sure seem to know what you're doing," Eva couldn't help saying. She idly wondered how many women he'd had sex with, and then mentally slapped herself. *You know better than to go there*, she thought, annoyed with herself.

"It's easy when it's with you," he said, but then he frowned.

"What?" Eva asked as a trickle of unease slipping through her. *Don't make problems where there aren't any,* she told herself, but it didn't help. Why the hell was he frowning right after they'd done the deed? She glanced down, wishing they weren't on top of the comforter. Suddenly she wanted to cover up her jiggly stomach. "Is something wrong?"

Charlie shook his head. "No, nothing. Nothing's wrong." He smiled at her again.

Eva stared at him, but he seemed okay. She didn't know what that frown had been about, but she took a deep breath and talked herself out of worrying about it. *I'll probably obsess over it later, but right now, I deserve to enjoy the afterglow,* she told herself, like a grownup. Because she was an adult woman, and she'd just had sex, and it had been awesome. She wasn't going to spoil it by acting like a petulant teenager.

"I've got a sudden craving for burgers. And beer," Charlie said, tucking her head below his chin where she couldn't see his expression.

"I have some in the freezer," Eva suggested, glad she'd done a grocery run that morning. The butterflies in her stomach didn't quite settle, but they faded a bit.

"Sounds like a date," Charlie said, yawning. The arm around her waist grew heavier as his muscles relaxed.

Well, he can't be too upset about anything if he's on the verge of falling asleep. Eva smirked. She'd heard that men tended to conk out after sex, and lo and behold, it seemed to be true. "Nap first, then food," she told him, closing her eyes, too.

Charlie murmured incoherently, and the next thing Eva knew, she had two hundred and some pounds of snoring male slumped against her. She didn't mind.

She didn't mind at all.

Chapter Eight

The next morning, Charlie drove to work late for the first time since he'd founded his construction company with his cousin. *And RJ is sure to tease me about it until I threaten to pound him,* he thought, pressing his lips together at the idea of having to explain what he'd done. RJ would probably be elated that Charlie had finally met someone he could fall in love with, but what the hell did he know? The man was divorced. His kids were all grown up. He was happily single, the bastard. He wasn't in danger of falling for someone over a decade his junior.

Charlie shook his head, dispelling the negative thoughts. He should be happy. He'd gotten laid for the first time in forever, with a girl he really liked, even if she *was* too young for him. He'd woken up in Eva's bed early enough to get to work on time, but her sleepy warmth had distracted him, and they'd made love instead of getting up. When Eva had seen the time, she'd shrieked and dashed out the door, leaving him to lock up. It had been just as well. Saying goodbye would've been incredibly awkward, otherwise.

"I'm going to have to keep things low-key," he muttered, hoping to God she understood why he couldn't let himself get too serious with her. Eva had her whole life ahead of her, and she deserved some guy her own age. She deserved to love, and be loved, by someone who wasn't crusty and old and worn out. He snorted. Okay, so he wasn't quite worn out at thirty-five, but compared to her? Compared to her, he had one foot in the grave. *You shouldn't have touched her*, a voice in the back of his head accused.

Charlie grimaced, then pulled into the gravel lot that housed Greenwood Construction. He and RJ had started the company as an all-around contracting firm, but after they'd built a tiny home for a guy who lived in upstate New York, they'd ended up specializing in custom tiny homes and campers. He couldn't say he wasn't happy about it. He loved building things with his hands, and he loved making unique objects, and it had all sort of spiraled out from there. RJ, his older cousin, had been the guy who'd taught him most of what he knew about wood and metal, and he'd been all for it when Charlie had proposed the company idea to him. RJ's twin son and daughter worked for them, too, so he supposed it was a family company, of sorts. It wasn't what he thought he'd ever be doing after he quit the rat race as a financial analyst, but he certainly wasn't complaining about it.

"You are *so* late, Charlie!" RJ said, walking out of the large red barn. He stood the same height and carried the same kind of muscle as Charlie, but his short beard was almost entirely silver, and he was balding enough that he liked to wear a bandana on his head to keep the sun off his scalp. Today's pick was red. He propped a pair of shades on his head as the morning sunlight slanted across his face. "First time you've ever been late to work. You must've met a woman." RJ grinned, clearly joking.

He's going to keel over when I tell him it really was a woman, Charlie thought, half embarrassed and half amused. "Hey, RJ," he called, getting out of his truck. He slammed the door and leaned back against it, aiming for casual nonchalance about his late arrival. "You're looking particularly decrepit this fine Monday morning. How's that arthritis? Did you fall out of bed again this morning?"

"Decrepit? I'm only sixteen years older than you are, you little shit," RJ said, laughing. His light eyes caught the sunlight, making the hazel color look almost green.

Charlie rolled his eyes. "Yet, unlike you, I have all my hair. And I'm not exactly little." He pushed off from the truck and sauntered towards the barn. "How are we doing on the little red house?"

"Aiden and Sophie are already on the road with it. Delivery should happen late this afternoon," RJ said, walking with him.

"I never thought they'd end up working for us and liking it," Charlie said, heading for the long metal table set at the rear of the barn. He and RJ kept the plans for their work there, along with an old coffee maker. He tilted his head, contemplating a cup of caffeine, but then decided against it. RJ's coffee making skills were enough to scour the lining from his esophagus, and he wasn't in the mood for that kind of trauma today.

"Me neither," RJ said. "But it's nice having my kids working here. I like it. They're good people, which is a minor miracle consider the crazy that is their mother."

"I like it, too," Charlie said, still walking. He did *not* comment on RJ's ex. The less said about her the better. He still couldn't figure out why the man had hooked up with that woman in the first place. He stopped in the center of their barn, taking in the view. The cavernous space was open to the outside now that it was summer, and three different builds of various sizes were ongoing inside. He looked up, sighing as a couple of mourning doves fluttered down and out. They had a nest in the rafters. Seemed a weird sort of omen to him this morning.

"Those birds are going to shit on the work, you know," he said sourly, walking back to the work table. It was time to push Eva to the back of his head and get to work. Trouble was, his mind and body weren't cooperating. Her scent lingered on his shirt. He could still feel her smooth skin on his fingertips. *You've got it bad*, he told himself, rubbing his thumbs against his forefingers.

"Too bad. I am *not* shutting the barn doors in the summer," RJ retorted, following him. "We'd die of heat exhaustion within the hour, and you know it." He tapped a calloused finger on the latest plans. "Things are looking good. We're ahead of schedule. Should be good to go for that trip we have planned later this season."

Charlie stared down at the paperwork, but all he could think about was Eva. Eva and her delicious ass. Eva and her soft, gorgeous skin. Eva and her wet pussy. *Shit. Get a grip, man,* he told himself as his cock twitched. He did *not* need a hard-on at work, at his age.

"It's a woman, isn't it?" RJ asked, crossing his arms as he leaned a hip against the high table. "I've never seen you so distracted. Who is she?"

Charlie scowled as his heart tripped a few beats. How the hell did RJ know? "I don't know what you're talking about," he said, following the deny-deny-deny philosophy of life.

"Please. I've known you since you were in diapers." RJ grinned.

"Ugh. Don't remind me," Charlie said, poking a finger at the plans on top of the pile. "Did we start on this one yet?"

RJ huffed and snatched the sheet out from under Charlie's hand. "We *finished* that one last week. That's the one the twins are out delivering, remember?"

Charlie frowned. He remembered. Really. He was just a little distracted.

"What's her name?" RJ asked as he rearranged the papers on the table.

"No one," Charlie said immediately. He had to head this off at the start, or he'd never hear the end of it.

"That's a unique name. How do you spell it?" RJ asked, eyes twinkling.

He's such a jerk. Charlie gave him a look. RJ stood there, smiling back at him amiably as if he wasn't needling his cousin for kicks.

"You realize you have a—" RJ broke off and waved at the side of Charlie's neck.

"A what?" Charlie asked, annoyed. He put his hand on his neck. *Ah, hell,* he thought, feeling his cheeks heat up. He hadn't considered that Eva might give him a love bite. He hadn't thought about much of anything except sinking into her tight heat. Neither of them had been thinking this morning, damn it.

RJ smirked. "You really want me to say it out loud?"

"For Christ's sake, RJ—" Charlie began, but his cousin cut him off.

"A hickey. A love bite. A big, whopping, giant—"

Charlie flushed. "All right. I get the picture." *Shit. I must have missed it when I showered, not that I could've done anything anyway,* he thought. It wasn't like he was going to put on a turtleneck in the middle of the summer. His hands twitched, but he refused to poke at his neck anymore. There wasn't anything to feel, anyway.

"Who's the girl?" RJ asked, folding his arms across his chest again. He leaned a hip against the table insouciantly. "And don't try to lie to me. I could read you when you were a kid, and I can read you now."

If he starts whistling, I'll have to punch him, Charlie thought, disgusted. They stared at each other for a moment, but then Charlie caved. If he didn't, they'd be here all damn day. RJ was like a dog with a bone when he sensed something juicy. "Her name is Eva," he muttered, wondering if RJ remembered her. He leaned back against the table, too, so he wouldn't have to look his cousin in the eye. *Damned family. Can't live with them; can't live without them.*

"Eva?" RJ stood up, eyebrows rising. "Little Eva Ruston? Phil's little girl? You're shitting me, right? Isn't she, like, twelve?"

Fuck. I guess he remembers her. Charlie scowled. "No, she's not twelve. She's a grown woman, you asshole," he told RJ, thinking again of Eva's amazing curves. She had a waist that was made for his hands. Tits that were made for his lips. And, lest he forget, she was also fourteen years younger than he was. *I am so screwed it isn't even funny.*

"She is?" RJ scratched at the stubble on his chin. "Huh. I guess you're right. She's living in that house all alone now, isn't she? Poor girl. I suppose she's technically a grownup, though," he said, looking thoughtful for a moment, and Charlie really thought he was going to be cool about it, but then the man had to ruin it. He grinned at Charlie. "She's a baby adult. You're about a thousand years older than she is, aren't you?"

Charlie pushed off from the table and strode to the newest build so he wouldn't strangle his cousin. "It's nothing serious." It couldn't be, after all. He was too old for her. She needed someone young. Someone who wouldn't keel over dead on her when she hit middle age. And, too, he wasn't really the commitment type. He'd been happily single his whole life. One little blip on the radar wasn't going to change that.

"Uh huh. Not serious." RJ trailed Charlie, then watched him strap on a utility belt. "Because you always get this defensive when it's 'not serious'." He used air quotes to emphasize the words. "You're funny when you're all riled up, Charlie."

Charlie tossed him a disgusted look.

RJ backed up a step, hands raised. "Just saying."

"She's too young for me," Charlie told him, picking up a sanding block. He started in on one of the cabinets he'd glued together last week. "She says she doesn't care about the age difference, but she's too young to know what it means. She doesn't understand the consequences."

"And did you tell her that?"

Charlie nodded. "Yeah. Of course."

RJ's eyebrows flew up. "You're crazy, Charlie. You don't tell a woman that she doesn't understand something. That's just asking for trouble." RJ laughed. "Damn. She must have been *pissed*." He picked up another sanding block and helped Charlie smooth out the side of the cabinet.

Charlie shrugged. "She wasn't pissed when I left this morning." Even though he knew he should keep his mouth shut, he had to brag just a little bit. He hadn't had a girlfriend in years. He hadn't felt like *this* in, well, ever.

RJ hooted. "You dog!"

Charlie scowled, angry with himself. "It's not like that," he told his cousin. He cursed himself internally for being an ass. Eva deserved better from him. He wasn't going to be her one and only forever guy, but the least he could do was not be a disrespectful jerk. Luckily, he knew RJ was only teasing. His cousin was a nice guy. One of the nicest guys he knew, actually.

"You seem awfully confused about *what*, exactly, *it* is," RJ pointed out, sanding steadily.

Charlie dropped his block on the table. "What *it* is, is a disaster. I'm an idiot, RJ. I should never have touched her." He raked his hands through his hair. "She told me that she had never been kissed. Never been on a date, and then she asked me to kiss her. To show her what it was like." He pinched his nose between his thumb and forefinger, frustrated that his body still found that hot as hell. He'd loved being Eva's first guy. He'd love being the one to show her how good it could be. "And then one thing led to another. I knew better, but I went ahead and did it anyway." Charlie stared at the cabinet. His hands were covered with sawdust. He couldn't bring himself to meet his cousin's gaze. "I'm so screwed, RJ. I don't want to hurt her, but she's so damned young. She needs someone her own age."

RJ stopped sanding and looked at him. "If I remember right, Eva lost both her mother and her father in a few short years. And she managed to finish college anyway, and now she supports herself. She sounds like the kind of woman who knows exactly what she wants, and if that person is you, maybe you should grab on to her with both hands and thank your lucky stars instead of pretending that you aren't falling hard." He gave Charlie a hard look. "Maybe *you're* the one who isn't grown up enough."

Charlie sighed. "She's young, RJ. Really young."

"And you're, what? Thirty-four? Thirty-five? And you think that's old?" RJ made a disgusted sound in the back of his throat. "I'm fifty-one, Charlie, and I've seen some shit. You know that. My ex was some kind of crazy. I raised two kids by myself." He shook his head. "And your Eva has seen some shit, too, and come out the other side intact. She's not a girl, not at her age, and certainly not after what she's been through. She's a grown woman, and that's a fact, no matter that I enjoyed busting your balls over the age difference." He snorted. "And here you are, trying to talk yourself into being an asshole. Don't do it. I might just have to smack you upside the head if you keep it up. I'm not too old to kick your ass, you know."

"I just want what's best for her," Charlie said, irritated. He wasn't an asshole. He wasn't trying to become one, either. He was simply trying to protect Eva from things she didn't know. From *him*. "I want her to be happy."

RJ started sanding again. "And you think that you making the decision about a relationship *for* her will do that? Huh. Interesting. Because it always works out so well when a man tries to make a woman's mind up for her." He started whistling.

Charlie scowled, but got to work, and fortunately RJ didn't say anything more.

****

Eva waited until the elevator doors at her office opened before allowing herself a tiny, little, indulgent freak-out. She was late for work, but that wasn't what had her heart pounding in her chest. It was the memory of Charlie sliding his gorgeous cock inside her this morning, and the look in his eyes as he did it that had her overwhelmed and excited. *And Kyra is going to see it all over me the moment I step through these doors,* she thought, watching them open.

Sure enough, the moment she sat down at her cubicle, Kyra sped over, all bright eyed and bushy tailed. "So? How did the date go?"

Date? What? Eva thought, confused for a moment, and then she remembered the guy who'd run screaming from her in the restaurant. Eva swiveled around in her chair to face Kyra and scowled. "Your guy took one look at me and booked it out of the cafe. Thanks for nothing, Kyra," she said, in full attack mode. Maybe if she was aggressive enough, Kyra wouldn't notice her happy sex flush.

"He did what?" Kyra's eyebrows rose. "Seriously? But what about—" She pursed her lips and pointed to Eva's neck.

Eva stared at her, confused. "What?" She put a hand on her neck, but didn't feel anything. What did that terrible date have to do with her neck?

"You have a hickey," Kyra said, laughing. She snorted as Eva flushed, and then, out of nowhere, Kyra sneezed all over her.

"Oh, ugh!" Eva wiped her face. Kyra had impeccable aim. "That's it. You are not my friend any longer. Gross." She grabbed a tissue from her desk and thrust it at Kyra. "Wipe your nose."

"I'm sorry! I'm sorry. It's just my allergies," Kyra said, clutching the tissue. "Anyway, that's not nearly as interesting as your hickey. Who, what, where, when, how?" she asked, eyes bright. "If the guy my mom set me up with ditched you, which, by the way, was a serious asshole move, how on Earth did you get a hickey?"

Eva glared at her friend. "The guy you twisted my arm into meeting for you told me I was too tall. Story of my life. I am never going on one of your dates for you again." *Not that I would anyway, now that I'm with Charlie,* she thought, and a little spasm of happiness tripped her heart again. She pushed the tiniest bit of unease down into the darkest recesses of her brain. Charlie had been lovely this morning. So what if he still insisted she was too young for him? It was too late now. He had her, but more importantly, *she* had *him*, and she wasn't about to give him up. Not now. Maybe not ever.

"Yes, yes, he was a jerk. I don't care. *Focus,* Eva," Kyra said impatiently, snapping her fingers. "The hickey? Explain, before I lose my mind."

"Your inability to control your curiosity isn't my problem," Eva said, shrugging. She tried to play it cool, but her friend's expression told her she'd failed, big time.

"I swear to God, Eva—" Kyra began, but Eva cut in before she could work her way into a full-blown tizzy.

"Fine! Fine, I'll tell you," Eva said, chewing on her lower lip. Kyra put her hands on her hips impatiently. Eva sighed. "Okay. So, you know that guy I like? Friend of my dad's? He came over to clean out the back gutters on Sunday. It was pouring. I had a massive leak into my living room."

"Wait, wait, wait," Kyra said, her voice rising higher with every "wait". "You mean that giant dude, Charlie Green-something? The investment guy?" Kyra's eyes went wide.

"He's not an analyst anymore. He started a boutique carpentry business with his cousin. They build tiny houses and redo campers and stuff like that," Eva said. She didn't know what Charlie retiring from his first career had to do with anything. It didn't matter to her. She loved Charlie for *Charlie,* not because of what he did for a living. Her friend, however, looked like she was about to keel over from astonishment. "And yes. Charlie Greenwood. He's nice." Even as she said the words, she winced. Her friend never went for "nice".

"Nice? Uh-huh. What*ever*." Kyra flapped her hand. "You're talking about the hot-as-hell dude who is, like, six feet ten, and built like a brick wall? Not to mention he's a zillion years older than you? Mr. Silver Fox guy? The one you've been crushing on since forever? That guy?"

"He's not *that* tall," Eva said defensively. She *liked* that he was tall. She didn't ever have to worry about him being all weird about her height. Charlie was tall enough and strong enough to *pick her up,* and that was only one of his many amazing qualities.

"Well, not for *you,* Ms. Amazon," Kyra retorted. "But for us mere mortals, he's a bit intimidating." She tilted her head. "I can't even imagine having sex with a dude like that. He could probably break me in two with one hand." She smirked. "He must have a ginormous cock."

Eva glared. "He's taken," she said curtly, images of said cock dancing through her brain. He *was* a tad large, not that she had anything to compare him to except her toys. "Taken by me, Kyra," she added, just to make things clear. "And he's not intimidating at all. He's the perfect height, if you ask me." *And he likes that he can let go with me, because I'm* not *tiny,* she reminded herself. She remembered the way he'd picked her up, as if she weighed nothing, and flushed.

Kyra laughed. "Easy, girl. I'm not after your man. I'm just after the details." She grinned impishly. "The juicer the better."

Eva spun around in her chair, giving her friend her back. There was no way she could deal with Kyra with the memory of Charlie going down on her fresh in her mind's eye. "Go away, Kyra. I'm not kissing and telling."

Kyra propped a hip on her desk, making it impossible for Eva to ignore her. "Seriously, though, Eva. Are you okay?" She asked, smoothing a hand down her pink and black patterned pencil skirt. "This guy is really is a lot older than you. He didn't hurt you, did he?"

Hurt me? Charlie? Eva glanced up, confused. Kyra was frowning, and Eva read genuine concern in her eyes. "I'm fine. Charlie is wonderful," she said quietly, thinking of all the ways he'd made her feel special. She especially liked the way he'd let her drive their lovemaking, always checking in with her before he did anything, and never pushing her beyond her comfort zone. "He gets me, Kyra. And he's not too big for me, and he's definitely not too old, even though he thinks he is. He tried to tell me that I should find someone my own age." She frowned, still annoyed over *that* particular weirdness. Weren't men *supposed* to like younger women? "Which is ridiculous. After everything I've been through, I can't really relate to younger guys. They're shallow. They don't understand what's really important in life."

Kyra swung her leg. "I know," she said, finally dropping her gossipy persona and letting the bestie that Eva loved peek out. "That's why I'm always trying to fend off my mother's matchmaking. She picks guys that don't understand me. She has no idea what I want, or what's important to me. I'm not looking for some rich husband." She shook her head. "I want someone I can relate to."

"And it's frustrating, right?" Eva asked, seeing that her friend got it. "And more importantly, all those other guys can't relate to *me*. I'm always too tall, too fat, or too smart for them. But Charlie is taller, bigger, and he might be just as smart as I am." Eva allowed herself a tiny grin at how he'd react to that statement. He'd probably laugh and argue that he was smarter, and Eva would argue back, and then they'd end up in bed again. He really was her perfect guy. If only he'd realize it, and stop pretending that what they had was temporary.

"You seem really happy, Eva," Kyra said, standing up. "And you know that if you're happy, I'm happy." She frowned. "But," she said, raising a finger. "If he hurts you, it doesn't matter how big he is. I'll have to kick his ass, and it won't be pretty."

Eva shook her head, smiling as she pictured her tiny friend trying to kick Charlie. The image was ludicrous. "He won't. I won't let him." She sat back in her chair. "You know me. I won't let him do that."

Kyra just huffed, and then stalked off to her desk. Her confident swagger was somewhat broken by another explosive sneeze. *It had* better *be allergies,* Eva thought, amused, and still somewhat grossed out. *If it isn't, I may have to kick* her *ass.*

****

It wasn't allergies.

Eva reclined on her sofa on Friday night, blowing her nose and coughing into a quickly disintegrating tissue as she dialed Charlie's number. It hadn't even been a week since she and Charlie had made love for the first time, and here she was. Sick. If Kyra were standing in front of her, Eva would be tempted to smack her for not covering her mouth when she'd sneezed all over her. She'd had plans for the weekend, and they didn't involve hacking up a lung.

"Eva? Hey, how are you feeling? Any better? What did the doctor say?" Charlie asked when he answered her call.

"I can't make it to dinner, Charlie. I'm sick as a dog," she rasped into her phone, grimacing at the finger-smudged screen. She'd have to disinfect it, along with everything else in her entire house. She had the plague. She'd been to see the doctor and had the antibiotics to prove it, since the stupid virus Kyra had given her had turned into a weird bacterial thing in her throat in record time. Who in the hell got this sick in only a few days' time? "It actually hurts to talk. The doctor told me it's strep on top of the cold virus, of all things. Ugh."

"Oh honey, that's terrible," Charlie said, concern evident in his tone. "I'll bring soup when I come over later."

"No!" Eva cringed, thinking of how awful she

looked. "You really don't have to," she said, wishing she were one of those women who looked pretty and luminous and tragic while sick. She wasn't. She was the kind of girl who looked like she had leprosy. "I won't be any fun to hang with. And you don't want to catch this. Trust me, Charlie." She coughed into her tissue again. "You *really* don't want to catch this."

He laughed. "If I was going to catch it, I would've caught it sometime this week. I've been at your place every night, remember?"

Eva flushed, which was quite a feat, considering that her fever already had her all hot and bothered. "I remember," she whispered, giving up on her voice altogether. She'd been coughing since Monday night, but they'd both thought it was just a regular cold virus. Last night she'd been so tired they hadn't done anything more than cuddle on the couch. When she'd woken up the next morning, she'd discovered that Charlie had carried her to bed and tucked her in. She had no memory of him doing it, and then he'd left her a cute note and a glass of orange juice on her nightstand. If she hadn't already been in love with him, that would've done it for her. And then she'd tried to stand up and had found out that she was way sicker than she'd thought. She'd had to stay home from work. *And even after all that, he still insists that he's too old for me, and this is a short-term thing. Ha. He's deluding himself*, she thought, warmed by his concern.

"I'm coming over, and I'm taking care of you, and you're not going to argue with me," Charlie said firmly. "I'll bring you some chicken soup. And you'll eat it."

This isn't the argument I want to have, she thought, wiping her nose again. *I'd rather fight over who gets to be on top next time.*

"Eva?"

"Okay, fine," she said, giving in way too easily. But honestly, she didn't have the energy to disagree with him. She felt like crap, and Charlie always made her feel better. "I like chicken soup," she rasped, then coughed again.

"Oh, baby. You sound like an old woman with a three pack a day habit," he laughed softly. "Hang in there. I'll see you soon." Charlie disconnected the call before she could say anything.

I'm not old. Eva stared at her cell phone's screen. *Okay, then. He claims he doesn't want me to get attached, and then he takes care of me while I'm sick. Typical male logic, my mom would say,* she thought, smiling fondly. *He has no idea how much he already cares, the big idiot.* She let her phone fall onto the cushions and closed her eyes. She woke sometime later to the sound of her front door opening.

"Charlie?" He was the only one besides herself who had a key. *It had better be Charlie, and not my creepy uncle.* She hadn't heard a peep from Albert since Charlie had run him and his sleazy friend off, thank God. She struggled to sit up, then gave up as a wave of vertigo swamped her. "Oh, ugh," she said, then grimaced. Her throat hurt like hell.

"The one and only," Charlie said, kicking the door shut with his foot. "Who else would it be? I'm the only one with a key to your house." He was juggling two bags of food, and from the scent, Eva could tell one of them held chicken soup. He smiled at her when their gazes met. "Hey, there, sweetheart. How are you doing?"

"Hey, Charlie," she whispered, making a face at the pain in her throat. She tried to sit up again, but he frowned at her.

"Don't you dare get up." He dropped a kiss on her head on his way to the kitchen. "I'll get you something that'll make it easy to eat on so you don't have to come to the table."

Eva watched him head for her kitchen. Five minutes later he reemerged with a tray. He set it on her coffee table and helped her sit up.

"I'm sorry to be such a bother," she said.

"You're not a bother. You're sick," Charlie said, handing her a spoon. "Eat as much as you can. I'll take care of everything else."

Eva sighed, but then he gave her a look. She gave in and started eating. A half hour later, she'd managed to consume three-quarters of her soup and a few crackers. Her throat still felt like someone had run sandpaper over it. "Thanks, Charlie."

"Of course," he said, setting his empty soup carton on the tray. "I'll clean this up in a minute. You just sit tight, okay?"

Eva nodded, watching Charlie stuff the rest of his sandwich into his mouth. *I really wish I weren't sick. It's not every day that a hot guy waits on me hand and foot. What a wasted opportunity*, she thought, feeling sorry for herself. She coughed, then blew her nose again. She felt a little better, enough to realize Charlie looked tired. He was wearing jeans and a t-shirt with his company logo on it, so she knew he'd come straight from work. He'd told her a couple days ago that he and his cousin were trying to finish up a tiny home for a client, and he'd been working late all week. A stray bit of sawdust still clung to his sleeve, and she wished she were well enough to brush it off for him. "I hate that you have to see me like this."

"It's no big deal, honey. Everyone gets sick." Charlie gathered up the soup she hadn't been able to finish, and balled up his empty sandwich wrapper, then tucked a stray curl behind her ear. "You need rest, Eva.

Just try and get some sleep." He stood up then, and went to the kitchen to dispose of the mess.

She sighed. "I'm tired of resting." Her voice came out half whisper, but she knew he heard her.

He smiled at her after he came back to the living room. "I know you're tired of resting, baby. Being sick sucks."

"I'm not a baby," she said, annoyed. He always said that, and most of the time she knew he didn't mean anything by it, but this time she couldn't help thinking of how much he hated their age difference. Having him call her "baby" just emphasized that he was more than a decade older than she was. And it shouldn't matter. She was an adult, dammit! But she wanted to be a *healthy* adult, so she could strip off his clothes and have her way with him, and instead she was sitting on the sofa wearing her ratty old sweatshirt and mismatched socks. The truth was that despite her bold words to Kyra, somewhere deep inside, she was afraid that he wouldn't stick around for very long. She wanted to savor him for as long as she could. *Everyone leaves me eventually,* she mused, head pounding as images of her parents' funerals danced through her thoughts. She really *was* sick if she couldn't keep her shit together. Usually she did much better than this. Eva rubbed her forehead, frustrated.

"Hey, stop that," Charlie said, putting a finger to the wrinkle between her brows. "I don't know what you're thinking about, but you don't have to worry so much, Eva. Plus, your face could freeze like that, and then what would you do?" He winked at her.

She gave him a look that told him she wasn't in a flirty mood. "What are you, my grandmother? That's an old wives' tale." Eva grimaced, then coughed again. "Besides, I already scare people away with my height and fatness and whatever-itude. I'm amazed you've stuck around as long as you have."

"It's only been a week since we started this thing. I know it can't be forever, but it can be a little longer than that," Charlie said as he gathered her into his arms. "Don't fuss. I'm here, aren't I? Just relax. Try to get some sleep."

"But for how long?" she asked before she could stop herself. "How long will you be here?"

"Oh, honey," he murmured, running a soothing hand down her back.

She knew that he knew she wasn't asking about just this night. *I want to know how long he's going to stay for real. Forever? Two more weeks? A day?* she pondered, even as she hated the way her thoughts turned maudlin when she felt like shit. *Just go to sleep, girl,* she finally told herself. Charlie was here now, and he was holding her just right. She had a lot to be grateful for.

Eva was almost asleep when she heard Charlie's whispered answer to her question. "I'll be here for as long as I can, sweetheart."

That certainly isn't forever, is it? she mused.

The thought didn't soothe her at all.

Chapter Nine

For the next month, they slipped into a routine: Eva would come home from work to find Charlie hanging out in her kitchen. He liked to cook for her, and since his hours were flexible, he often surprised her with food. He made her laugh. He gave her back rubs when the long ride on the bus home twisted her spine into a pretzel. In return, she cooked for him on the weekends and dragged him out to the movies. More often than not he slept over, holding her in his arms the entire night. They never argued. They just … fit. They fit into each other's lives so perfectly she couldn't remember what it had been like without him there, in her house. In her heart. Falling in love with Charlie was so damned easy. How could she help it?

But then there were the times she'd catch him frowning seemingly at nothing, but whenever she asked him what was wrong, he'd smile and say nothing. Often, she'd wake up late at night to find him standing at her window, staring out into the darkness, and she'd realize that he'd waited until she fell asleep and then left the bed. When she asked him why, he simply said he couldn't sleep, but she knew that wasn't why he kept his distance from her. He didn't like how good they were together. He didn't like the way they just fit together so easily. He was afraid. She could feel it, deep in her bones.

And he never invited Eva over to his house.

Oh, she'd been there before, when her parents were still alive. She remembered the soaring ceilings and gorgeous wood walls of his private cabin set in the middle of God only knew how many acres of woodland. His place was a testimony to privacy, built for a very private man. And somehow, she knew that by coming over to *her* house all the time, he was saying something about the impermanence of this thing between them. It made her ache. It felt like he was breaking her heart very slowly, in tiny little increments, which was so strange, because she'd also never been happier in her life.

And then, on a Monday morning a little over two months after they'd begun this *thing* that Charlie was afraid to label, and that she called her Hot Daddy Fling just so she could watch Charlie squirm, Eva lifted her head out of the toilet and cursed her life. What the hell had happened to her damned birth control? Dread filled her as she swallowed the rising bile. She would *not* barf again. She refused. *Or at least not again this morning. Maybe this afternoon*, she told herself. She frowned, then leaned over the toilet again, trying to dry heave quietly. When she was done, she rinsed her mouth.

"And now I'm going to be late for work. Again." She impatiently shoved her hair back as she swallowed back another wave of nausea. It was settling down, thank God. She had just enough time to shower before catching her bus into the city. She didn't have time to pee on the pregnancy test she'd bought yesterday, but it didn't matter. She'd already peed on two others yesterday morning.

"Eva? You okay?" Charlie called from the bedroom.

Perfect timing, as always. She grimaced. "How about no?" she muttered under her breath.

"Eva? It's getting late," he called louder, as if she hadn't heard him before.

"Just brushing my teeth!" she replied, thinking about the tests she'd wrapped back up in the shopping bag and shoved in the back of her bathroom cabinet behind the shower cleaner. She didn't want him to know. Mr. This Is Just Temporary would totally freak. She glanced at the door, then swallowed hard as another wave of bile—or was it terror?—threatened to scald her esophagus. "God damn it," she said bitterly, bending over to spit toothpaste.

By the time Charlie opened the door, she'd recovered enough to smile at him and take the bagel he offered her. "I've got to go on that business trip tomorrow," he reminded her. "It's been set up for months, or I would've scheduled it differently." He made a face. "Sorry."

She frowned, then nodded. "Oh, that's right. I almost forgot." She hadn't forgotten. She just hadn't wanted to think about it, so she'd pushed it to the back of her mind.

"I'll only be gone a week. Two at the most, hopefully," he told her, leaning in to kiss her.

Eva smiled at him as he pecked her cheek, and then took a bite of her bagel. He'd toasted it and added cream cheese, just the way she liked, carbs be damned. Since Charlie didn't seem to mind the extra weight around her hips and belly, she'd stopped obsessing so much over her food. And that had been why she'd thought she'd put on a few pounds.

"Sweet," he said, licking his lips, as if her cheeks were candy.

Eva rolled her eyes, outwardly smiling, while inwardly she railed against fate. *I'm not fat because I'm eating bagels,* she thought, barely controlling her panic. *I'm fat because I'm pregnant with Charlie's love child. I'm a fucking cliché.* Luckily for her, the weird morning sickness thing only happened once she got up, and mostly when she was trying to brush her teeth. So, it had been easy to hide it from him. She knew she couldn't go on like this forever, but she'd only just realized what had happened! Right? *And I don't want him to worry*, she told herself, all the while knowing she was just making excuses.

Charlie grinned at her, then handed her a travel mug of coffee. "I know you hate bringing this onto the bus, but you were in the bathroom so long that you're out of time."

She blinked at him, then took the coffee she could no longer drink. Caffeine was supposed to be bad for babies, wasn't it? "Thanks, Charlie." Why did he have to be so damned amazing? He really was an awesome boyfriend, except for the whole "I'm too old for you" thing.

He shrugged, then gave her a smoldering look. "It's the least I could do. It's my fault we're late." In his tight jeans and tight t-shirt, that kind of expression could set a woman's panties on fire in less than a second.

Eva was *not* immune. She blushed, then shook her head, annoyed that he could still make her feel like a fluttering virgin. "I didn't mind." He'd woken her up with his mouth on her pussy, and what woman could say no to that on a Monday morning? *Dammit. He's basically perfect, except for his obsession over our age difference,* she thought, wishing she could tell him about the baby.

But she couldn't. He'd probably offer to marry her. And then instead of living happily ever after, he'd feel trapped. And resentful. And then they'd get divorced and she'd end up a single mom, juggling child care and joint custody, and slowly growing to hate him for being such an idiot.

A therapist would say you're fortune-telling and catastrophizing, Eva told herself, but she couldn't make herself see past her terror. Not yet. Maybe not ever.

"You ready to go?" Charlie asked her, picking up his laptop bag. He'd actually brought work home last night, for the first time, and he'd already packed clothes for his trip into his truck. Once again, he'd managed to do all of this without Eva having the slightest clue until he'd told her about it after the fact. It was as if he had an entirely separate life from what they did together. Which kind of sucked. She sighed, trying not to think about it, but her brain wouldn't let it go. While Charlie was here, he was *here*, and Eva never felt left out or distant, but she couldn't help but think that he'd closed a door, somehow, when she wasn't looking. A door she didn't have a key to. A door she wanted to open in the worst way, because she had a feeling that inside the room beyond was everything she'd ever wanted in her life.

"Eva? You okay?" Charlie cupped her cheek. His light brown eyes twinkled at her fondly.

He has no clue. Eva didn't know how the hell she was going to do this without him. She had to call the doctor. She had to decide what came next in her life, and it terrified her. And she had to do all of it alone. *Get a grip, girl. You've been alone before and you managed,* she told herself as she smiled brightly at him. "I'm fine. I'm ready."

****

Charlie smiled as Eva waved him off, but as soon as his truck turned the corner, the happy expression slid off his face. He had to do something. What, he didn't know, because he sure as hell didn't want to break it off with her, but this thing between them had grown way out of proportion to what he'd intended.

And if you break it off with her, you're going to be a giant asshole, he mused grimly, not to mention that he didn't really *want* to break it off. Why? Because nothing was wrong. Eva was perfect. She was his perfect woman: funny, brilliant, and so fucking gorgeous it made his heart ache in all the best ways. There was absolutely nothing wrong with anything, except that she was too fucking young for him, and *that* would never change. Not today, not tomorrow, and he sure as hell couldn't ignore the past. So, he had to break it off for her sake. "Because she's too fucking young for you, old man," he said, savagely gunning the engine. The truck practically flew up the exit ramp to the interstate.

The guilt that crawled up his spine almost every night was enough to keep him from sleeping. And Eva had noticed. He knew she had. And now he was lying to her about why he stood at her window, staring into the yard his best friend had planted and cared for. His *dead* best friend. Whose daughter Charlie was fucking, deliriously, every night and sometimes in the morning and afternoon, too, damn it all to hell.

"You're going to hell, and you're going to deserve every moment you spend there," he muttered, and then he firmly shut the door on those thoughts. He had work to do, and agonizing over something he couldn't change wasn't going to help him in any way.

It wouldn't help Eva, either.

****

"How's the little lady?" RJ asked later that day. They were driving together up to Maine, and of course the traffic on I95 was as hellish as ever.

Charlie mentally ground his teeth at the question. Maybe if he didn't answer, RJ would let it drop. He pretended to hum along with the song on the radio. Truth was, he had no idea what the hell was playing.

"You've been really quiet about her lately."

Or maybe he won't let it drop. Charlie shrugged, deliberately nonchalant. If RJ picked up on his unease, he'd be like a dog with an old bone: relentless and annoying. "She's fine."

RJ made an "hmm" sound under his breath.

HOW LONG IS FOREVER?

"What?" Charlie glanced at his cousin, irritated. Why couldn't the man just let it be? *Oh, yeah. Because my life is never that simple, that's why.*

"It's just that I've noticed you've been really happy the past few months. Happy like I've never seen you before," RJ told him, flicking the radio dial to a different station. A blaring rap song burst through the speakers, and Charlie slapped RJ's hand away and switched it back to his country music preset. "And then all of a sudden, you've suddenly become a cranky old man, which is kind of weird, considering you're practically a baby, compared to me," RJ added, settling back into his seat. "What gives? Did she dump you?"

"No," Charlie said tersely. How could he possibly explain to his friend how he was the one fucking it all up?

"Please tell me you're not still obsessing over the age thing," RJ said, tapping the passenger window control. Up. Down. Up. Down. Outside, the traffic inched forward. An emergency vehicle passed them in the access lane on the right, lights flashing.

"For God's sake, stop with the fidgeting, RJ," Charlie said, exasperated. "You're killing me, here." He wished he could set this entire interstate on fire, and all the traffic with it. Why the hell did people drive like idiots? He supposed the poor suckers in the crash up ahead were thinking the exact same thing.

"So you *are* obsessing over the age thing. Or is it fear of commitment?" RJ leaned in and peered at Charlie's face.

"Stop it," Charlie growled, pushing him away.

RJ ignored him, leaning forward again to jab a finger in Charlie's face. "You, my friend, are an idiot."

Tell me something I don't know. Charlie scowled. "I'm screwing up her life. At first it was just a fling, but now…" He trailed off, not sure how to characterize what he and Eva had. A relationship? Sure. Yeah. A commitment? His entire psyche shied away from *that*. RJ had hit the nail on the head, like usual.

"But now it's gone way beyond fling status," RJ said, completing Charlie's sentence with his uncanny perceptiveness. "Why is that such a bad thing? Haven't you ever thought about settling down? Starting a family?"

A family implies children, which implies babies. Jesus. An image of Eva swollen with his child flashed through his head, and his dick twitched. The thought of her pregnant made him want to howl his possession of her to everyone. He'd have to marry her if that happened, and God help him if that thought didn't actually send a tiny burst of happiness shooting right through him. What the fuck was wrong with him? She was *too young*. She was *Phil's daughter*. Charlie tried to shrug the idea of marrying her away, but the image persisted.

"You could do a lot worse than Eva, you know," RJ added, clearly not done tormenting Charlie. "Have you ever actually considered what your life would be like without her? Seriously. Humor me and imagine how you'd feel if she was suddenly not there anymore. Imagine how you'd feel if she was dating some other guy."

I'd feel like pounding him into a bloody pulp. Charlie bit back a growl. The thought of Eva kissing someone else made him see red. The idea of her actually having sex with some other guy wasn't a thing he could contemplate with any sort of calm. And a future without being able to go over to her house and fold her into his arms was too grim to dwell on. His entire being cringed away from the image. Eva felt like home to him. She felt like the best thing that had ever happened to him.

HOW LONG IS FOREVER?

How did I get myself into this situation? he wondered as the sick, twisted feeling in the pit of his stomach grabbed hold of his lungs and squeezed them until he couldn't breathe right. *It wasn't supposed to be like this. I was supposed to teach her about sex, and then we were supposed to go our separate ways.* He rubbed his eyes, wishing he could rub some sense into his heart, but he'd finally realized that wasn't an option anymore. "Just … stop, okay? I can't talk about this right now, RJ."

"Are you picturing it?" RJ prodded, clearly trying to test Charlie's patience as he ignored his plea. "Can you see Eva with someone else's ring on her finger? Raising someone else's baby?"

Charlie decided to just lay it all out there. "I'm fucking my *dead best friend's daughter*, RJ. There's no way to sugarcoat that kind of bullshit," he said grimly. The guilt he felt was so thick he could almost chew on it, but his need for Eva was just as strong. He was so fucking *fucked*. "It's wrong. And it'll always *be* wrong, no matter what I want, or what Eva wants, or what anyone else thinks."

"So it's just fucking then, is it?" RJ asked, like the jerk he was. "Just a sweet bit of pussy, huh?"

Charlie tossed his cousin a glare. "Shut up, RJ. I swear to God, just shut it." He saw an exit up ahead and put on his turn signal. He'd go mad if he had to sit in this traffic for much longer, especially with his damn cousin spouting off like an idiot. The car in front of him finally moved a few feet, thank Christ.

"So, not just a sweet bit of—"

"*Don't* fucking say it, RJ," Charlie cut him off angrily. "You're family, and you're also my friend, but that won't stop me from decking you if I have to," he snarled, barely keeping his shit together. "It's not like that." He swerved to catch the exit, ignoring the horn blaring at him from behind as he cut off another driver with the same idea. He sped down the ramp to the traffic light, then took a right, not knowing and not caring where he was going. He'd find a gas station and stretch his legs a bit. Maybe find a back route out of this mess.

"What is it like, then?" RJ asked, obviously not a man who knew when the hell to shut up.

Jesus Christ. I'm going to kill him, and no one will blame me. Charlie pulled into a service station and slammed the truck into a parking space. Very carefully, he turned the key to shut off the engine. If he wasn't careful, he'd punch RJ in the face, and neither of them really wanted that. RJ didn't speak, thank God. They sat there for a minute that felt like an eternity, listening to the engine tick before Charlie finally screwed up the courage to answer his cousin.

"I think I'm going to have to marry her, RJ," he said quietly, and then he put his head in his hands.

****

Three hours later, Eva cursed herself for pretending she was okay. She needed a hug. She needed Charlie to stay home. Instead, she'd pecked him on the lips as he'd got into his truck, and then she'd walked to her bus stop, as if everything in her life was fine. It wasn't. It really, really wasn't fucking fine. She chewed her bottom lip, not caring that she'd already chapped it to the point of pain.

"Hey, girl! How's that hot silver fox boyfriend of yours?" Kyra asked, wandering over like she so often did in the morning. She wore a sleek, cream shift with red heels, and managed to look both professional and sexy. Eva didn't know how she pulled it off. She felt like lasagna that had been heated up three times—stale and totally unappetizing.

HOW LONG IS FOREVER?

"Is he still making all your dreams come true?"

Eva glanced at her friend, and then at the phone in her hand. She slowly put it down. She looked up at her friend, but her throat closed up before she could get any words out.

"Oh my gosh, what's wrong?" Kyra crouched down. Her dark eyes stared up at her with worry. "Eva?"

Eva shook her head. She'd just set up an appointment with her doctor. It made everything feel very, very real. How in the hell was she going to deal with this? For the first time in a long, long time, she actually felt too young for her life. She felt naive and stupid. How could she have forgotten that antibiotics wrecked birth control pills? That stupid cold virus, bacterial strep, fucking plague thing had sabotaged her up, down, and sideways. She bit her lip, hard enough to draw blood this time, in an effort to keep from crying.

"Oh, Kyra," she said, voice cracking. She twisted her hands together. She would *not* cry at work. She wasn't going to be that girl. *Right? Right.*

"Did that idiot break up with you?" Kyra asked gently, taking her hands. "I will so totally kick his ass, if you need me to. You know that, right? I am here for you, sister."

Eva looked down into her friend's kind brown eyes and burst into tears.

Chapter Ten

Eva looked at the notification on her phone, but declined the call. Again. Charlie had been unusually affectionate over the phone while he'd been away, especially since he'd had to extend his trip, but every time they talked, she could barely keep it together. She'd started not answering. So, he'd started texting. She'd resorted to turning her phone off while at work. She told him she was busy, but she didn't know if he was buying it. She wondered if he felt guilty that he'd had to stay away for longer than he'd promised. She missed him. His absence hurt her heart, even as she tried to convince herself that this time apart was a good thing. *And it* is *a good thing*, she reminded herself yet again. *You need this time to get your shit together, remember?*

"He still texting?" Kyra asked, sucking loudly at her smoothie. They were at lunch in the small deli across the street from their building. They'd gone later than usual to beat the busy noon hour, so they had a table to themselves for once.

Eva sighed. "This was a call, actually, but yeah. It's Charlie."

"Just tell him about the baby, Eva," Kyra said. She picked up her napkin and dabbed at the foam on her lip. "You're being an idiot."

No, I'm being a coward. That's worse. Eva shook her head, dismissing those thoughts. They weren't helping. "You don't understand, Kyra. He never wanted to be in a relationship with me. I'm *positive* he doesn't want to have a kid with me." She picked up her plastic fork and then set it back down. She really wasn't hungry. Wasn't being pregnant supposed to make you ravenous? Instead, she felt vaguely anxious and nauseated most days, and eating required a great deal of focus on her part, something she also lacked, lately.

Kyra nodded. "So, abortion?"

"What the heck, Kyra?" Eva recoiled, glaring at her friend. "No! Seriously? Do you even know me?" The thought of ending her pregnancy made her want to puke, and she'd already been doing enough of that. She imagined a baby with Charlie's eyes, and then had to swallow bile. No. No abortion for her. She didn't know what she was going to do yet, but it wouldn't be that. She might not be in an ideal situation to have a baby, but she'd figure something out. She always did. She stared at her friend, not surprised when Kyra's expression told her she was trying to goad Eva into talking. *Damn it. Best friends can be really annoying sometimes, especially when they're trying to help.*

"Ah." Kyra disingenuously propped her chin on her hand. "You've entered the world of Contradictory Hopes and Expectations. It's a fine place to wallow. Ask me how I know." She drank more of her smoothie through her straw, making an obnoxious sucking sound.

"You're disgusting, you know that?" Eva told her.

Kyra shrugged. "I'm not the one avoiding reality."

Eva rolled her eyes. "I don't know what I'm going to do yet, but it won't be an abortion, and you know that. You're just trying to get a rise out of me."

"I'm trying to make you stop wallowing and start thinking about your situation," Kyra said succinctly.

Eva scowled. Kyra was right. "I hate you."

"No, you don't."

"Are you sure about that?" Eva used her fork to push a crouton around her plate. She really didn't feel like eating today. Or yesterday. Or tomorrow. She eyed Kyra sourly. If she stabbed her friend, she wouldn't have to continue this conversation.

"Your options are to, A. tell him, B. tell him," Kyra said, ticking off points on her fingers. "And C. tell him." Her smile slipped from her face, and for a moment Eva could see her friend's seriousness poking through. Kyra always had a smart remark, but behind that facade, her heart was true. "It's his baby, too, you realize."

"I could move to Oregon," Eva said, poking at her salad again. She hated salad. Why did she order a salad? She especially hated raw onions, and they were all over this dismal plate of limp spinach and romaine. She missed bread. And cheese.

"Also, you need to eat again, sometime," Kyra pointed out, looking at Eva's plate. "Stop with the bunny food, Eva. You're eating for two, now. Get a damn burger, or something."

Eva's stomach growled. "Ugh." She thunked her head down on the table, annoyed with Kyra all over again. She knew that the other people in the little deli were staring, but she didn't care.

"Oh my God, this is ridiculous. You're being ridiculous," Kyra told her, snatching Eva's salad and tossing it in the trashcan behind her.

"Hey!" Eva crossed her arms over her chest. "I was eating that." She refused to admit she was relieved to see her sad little salad disappear.

"No, you weren't. You were playing with it like a ten-year-old trapped in a middle school cafeteria." Kyra stood up and gestured imperiously to the guy behind the deli counter. When he looked at her, she ordered a burger and fries.

"I thought you were a vegetarian," Eva said as her stomach growled again. She could totally eat a burger. Her midsection growled louder. *Yeah. A burger with cheese and a tomato,* she thought, suddenly ravenous. And then she remembered how much Charlie had enjoyed the burgers she'd made a few weeks ago and her growling stomach flipped directly to nausea. Again.

"I'm only a vegetarian when my mother is around so I don't have to argue with her, but that doesn't matter. This is for you," Kyra said, handing over money to the guy behind the counter. She grabbed the plate he handed her and plopped it down in front of Eva. "Here. Eat." Then, she sat down and picked up her smoothie again, arching a superior eyebrow at Eva. "Don't make me get the mustard."

I hate mustard. Eva stared at the burger. She really was hungry. "Shit, Kyra." She picked it up and started eating. "He's going to freak."

Kyra shrugged. "So what? What's the worst that could happen?"

Eva shook her head. Her mouth was full of delicious, amazing beef. Besides, Kyra knew everything she could say anyway. That was how best friends worked, even if Kyra was a pushy bitch sometimes.

"I mean, he's not the kind of guy that smacks you around, is he?" Kyra slid her empty cup to the center of the table.

Eva almost choked. "No! Never. He would never hit me. God, Kyra. He's *not* that kind of man." She determinedly took another bite of her meal.

Kyra pointed at her, dark eyes snapping. "I didn't think so. And that means you've gotta tell him. You're being stupid." She stood up.

Eva swallowed hurriedly. "Wait, where are you going?" She dabbed at her mouth with her napkin.

"I'm going to hang out with my friends who aren't dumb," Kyra said, and then she sauntered out of the deli.

Eva stared after her, and then looked down at her

half-eaten burger. "Well, shit."

****

Later that evening, Eva slid into her bathtub, sighing as the hot water seeped into her sore muscles. She'd read something about pregnancy hormones loosening tendons or something, and she believed it. She'd been tired and cranky and sore for the last few weeks, and it wasn't like she was hitting the gym or anything, because when she wasn't tired and cranky and sore, she was barfing. So far, everything about being pregnant sucked. She tipped her head back and sighed, not surprised when her phone rang. Again. She leaned over and grabbed it, then bit her lip before tapping "Accept". She had to stop this. Charlie had to know something was wrong. He might be commitment-phobic, but he wasn't an idiot.

"Hey, Charlie," she said trying to sound upbeat and failing. She winced. If *she* could hear the exhaustion in her voice, there was no way Charlie was going to miss it.

"Hey, sweetheart. You sound tired," he said. "Are you getting enough sleep?"

Eva smiled wryly. "Yeah. Sort of." She didn't elaborate. For a moment Charlie didn't speak, but just as the silence edged into awkward, he sighed.

"I have a feeling you've been avoiding my calls since I've been on this trip, Eva," he said quietly.

That's not a question, so I don't have to answer him, Eva told herself. *Right?*

Charlie continued. "I know I've had to stay away longer than I expected. We're having trouble with our main lumber supplier, so we've had to go further out to find new ones."

"I know. You told me." Eva closed her eyes, feeling tears well up again. She blinked them away. She refused to cry again. She'd been blubbering all this past week, and she was sick of herself. "It's okay," she said, then bit her lip. Charlie was sure to hear the anxiety behind her words. She could pretend that she didn't really hear the question hiding behind his explanation, but it prodded at her anyway. *Oh, Charlie. What are we doing?* she wondered, flexing her foot just at the surface of the water. Bubbles slid across the tub. She really didn't want to have this conversation.

Charlie paused, and when Eva didn't say anything more, he finally asked outright. "*Have* you been avoiding my calls, Eva?"

What could she say? *Yes, I've been avoiding your calls because I'm totally preggers and you're going to hate me for the rest of our lives and I completely dread it?* She gritted her teeth. Water sloshed at the edges of the tub as she involuntarily tensed up. "I haven't been feeling well. I'm just really tired lately." There. That wasn't a lie. Not exactly. Guilt pricked her. The burger she'd eaten earlier sat like a stone in her stomach.

"You work too hard, and I know how tiring that long commute in and out of the city is. Maybe you should take a few days off," Charlie said, voice low and steady. "I hate the thought of you working so much, baby."

Eva frowned as she heard rustling over the line. *What is he doing?* she wondered, trying not to let the sound of his voice lull her into comfort. She didn't deserve it. She was keeping one of the most important things you could tell a guy from Charlie because she was … what? Scared? Selfish? She shook her head. Those were terrible reasons. *You have to tell him.*

Charlie continued, clearly oblivious to her tortured thoughts. "I'll be home soon. Friday at the latest."

Eva let herself slide further down into the water. It was Wednesday night. She had less than two days to figure out what to do. She kicked a foot up, splashing her tile wall. Water and suds dripped down. She did it again. It was easier than making conversation while a giant fucking problem lodged itself up against her teeth like a damned barnacle. She didn't trust herself to not just blurt out "I'm having a baby," so she kept quiet.

"Are you taking a bath?" Charlie asked, a hint of amusement in his voice. "I hear water."

Eva flushed. "Uh. Yeah." What did *that* matter? Although she had to admit, she wasn't really used to talking to a man while naked. Yeah, sure, she and Charlie had been shagging like crazy, and he'd been acting the part of a doting boyfriend for the past few months, but it still felt weird. Did anyone ever get used to being part of a couple? *I don't suppose I'll ever know,* she thought sadly.

"That's ... hmm. Unexpectedly sexy." Charlie's voice dropped into a lower register. "Bubble bath?"

More of the same rustling sound as before came through the line as Eva flushed again. Out of nowhere, her quiescent libido woke up and informed her that the sound of her man talking over the phone in that particular tone of voice was extremely arousing. *Okay, what the hell?* She shifted in the water, biting her lip as the liquid swished around her body. *Whoa. Pregnancy hormones?* she wondered, even as she struggled to answer Charlie. "Uh, yes. It's a bubble bath. Vanilla scented, actually."

"Oh, baby," Charlie said softly. "You're naked, in a bubble bath, and I'm hundreds of miles away. This is a tragedy."

Eva giggle, despite her misery. How did he do that? How could he make her laugh, especially *now,* of all times, when she was stressing over things he had no idea about? "You're not missing much. I'm basically just soaking here." She smiled, despite herself. "I'm turning into a raisin. A wrinkly, ugly raisin."

"Honey, the thought of your magnificent breasts floating in a sea of vanilla foam is definitely not an ugly one, and if I were there, I'd make sure you realized that," Charlie said emphatically. "Put your phone on speaker and set it down somewhere safe."

"What?" Eva frowned through her blush. Magnificent breasts? She peered down at her boobs, then snorted. Her nipples had tightened with her arousal, and they really *did* look a bit like raisins, but she couldn't deny that Charlie sure as hell had a way with words. "Why?"

"Just do it."

She pursed her lips, then balanced her phone on the lip of the tub. If she was careful not to bump it, it would be fine. Over the line, she heard more rustling. What was he doing? It sounded like he was getting into bed. Or undressing. Or maybe both? A frisson of heat swept through her unexpectedly. Was he naked? Was he erect? She imagined Charlie's cock, hard and rosy at the tip, and maybe a little bit wet from wanting her.

"You there, baby?"

Eva startled, and then nodded, before remembering she had to speak. *He can't see you, dummy*, she reminded herself, biting her lip. "Of course I'm here. Where would I go?" She stuck a toe out of the water again. The bubbles tickled her skin.

Charlie chuckled. "Where indeed. Okay, Eva, I want you to touch yourself. Touch your nipples."

Eva's breath caught. "What?" Her fingers twitched. She wanted to touch herself. She really, really did.

"You heard me," Charlie said, a hint of command

in his tone. "Are your breasts soft and warm? Have your nipples pebbled up for me?" He mmm'd over the line. "I wish I was there. I'd put my mouth on them and suck them. Maybe bite them until you cry out. I know how much you like that." His voice firmed. "Touch yourself, Eva. Tell me how it feels."

Oh my God. He's phone sexting me, she thought, incredulous, but unbelievably turned on. *Do I dare?* Eva swallowed, then tentatively put a finger to her left nipple. "It feels smooth. Silky." She shivered. Her nipple had contracted into a tight, hard nub. She brushed her finger over it again.

"Pinch it." Charlie's voice was implacable. "Just the way I know you like."

"Charlie—" Eva began, voice rough, but he cut her off.

"Darling, I'm on my hotel bed, naked, imagining how sweet and soft you feel," he said in a heated voice. "I'm naked, and aroused. I have my hand on my cock, and I wish it was your hand. Or even better, your mouth." He inhaled, and Eva felt every iota of frustration evident in the sound. "Pinch your nipple for me."

Eva sucked in a breath and held it. Under her fingers, her nipple almost hurt. When she rolled it between her fingers, it sent sparks to her clit. She breathed out, shivering in the warm bathwater.

"You're touching yourself, aren't you?" Charlie asked. "So am I. My hand is so tight around my cock it hurts, and I wish it were your sweet cunny instead of my fingers."

Oh my God. Eva fumbled with the phone, pushing it further from the edge of the tub. With her luck, she'd kick it and it would fall into the water. She touched her nipple again. Was she really going to do this? Now? After being so scared and worried and stressed? *Hell, yes.*

"Eva?"

"Yes," she said, hearing the desire in her voice. *I'm having phone sex with Charlie,* she thought, almost desperate. "I'm touching my nipple," she said, breathless. She wanted this little diversion from real life. She *needed* it. *And if I lose him, at least I'll have this memory to hold onto.*

"Oh, baby. I've got my hand on my cock, but it doesn't feel like you. I'm not soft and hot and wet like you are," Charlie said roughly. "I'm not sweet."

Nothing about him is sweet. A thrill shot through Eva as she rolled her nipple between her fingers. "It doesn't feel the same without you here, either," she whispered. She could hear the need in her voice, and it made her blush.

"Touch your other breast," he said, and over the phone she could hear him clear his throat. "I'm imaging how rosy and perfect your nipples look. I can remember exactly how they feel on my tongue." He exhaled.

Eva gasped, pinching both nipples now. "Charlie—"

"I'm cupping my balls, Eva. I'm pretending that you're touching me, and my cock is so fucking hard right now." Charlie's voice had dropped completely into the lower register he used when balls-deep inside her.

That just did things to Eva. Sexy things. Dirty things.

"Touch your clit, honey," he said, almost growling. More rustling accompanied his order. "Tap it. Play with it the way I would if I were there."

Eva shuddered, but did as he asked, sliding her fingers down her body to her pussy. When her finger met the swollen bud, she swallowed. "Oh God," she said, circling the tip with a finger. She imagined what Charlie would do and slotted her clit between her fingers. The bubbles in the bathtub swirled around her arm. "It feels so good," she said, breathless.

"Does it?" Charlie asked softly. "As good as my mouth on you? As good as my teeth?"

Fuck, he's killing me. Eva so desperately wanted his mouth suckling her right now. Her finger moved faster as she shook her head. "No," she managed to say, still working at her clit. She couldn't stop now. Her orgasm fluttered just out of reach. Water sloshed at the edge of the tub, perilously close to her phone, but she didn't care.

"Good. I'm glad it doesn't feel the same," Charlie said, voice nothing but gravel and command. "Because I want you to miss me. I want you to miss the way it feels when I kiss you. When I give you my cock."

"I do," she said, voice trembling. She pinched her right nipple harder, and then dipped her finger deep into her cunny. "I wish you were here," she said, surprising herself, because she meant it. Even with the baby, and the doubt, she missed him desperately. She *needed* Charlie, much as it hurt to admit it. She didn't want to do this alone.

"Oh, me too, honey. I wish I was there to kiss you and suck on your beautiful, curvy tits, and fuck you until we both forget our names." Charlie's voice had gone quiet. "I'd fuck you with my cock until you screamed, and then I'd fuck you again. And then a third time, until we were both sore and exhausted."

Eva moaned out loud. She was close to orgasm, and that made no sense. She'd never been able to masturbate herself so easily.

"Are you still fucking yourself with your fingers, sweetheart?" Charlie asked her. He sounded out of breath.

Eva nodded as she imagined him jacking himself in a dark hotel room. "Yes. I'm still touching myself." She couldn't bring herself to say the word "fuck" to him, but he seemed to have no such problem. *But then, he's always been the one to say it during sex*, she thought, fingers moving faster. She pictured him looming above her: hard cock and body and laughing eyes as he slid into her. She moaned.

"Oh, baby, you sound so fucking hot," Charlie told her.

Eva moaned again. She couldn't help it. "Charlie, I wish you were here."

"Good," he said, voice ragged. "Because I'm fucking my hand, and pretending that it's you. I'm pretending that you have your pretty lips wrapped around my cock, and God!" He broke off. "God, I want you so bad. I *always* fucking want you."

Eva threw her head back as she played with her clit. She was swollen and so wet the water couldn't wash it away anymore. "So close," she gasped, and Charlie groaned.

"Me, too. I'm so fucking hard for you, baby, but I don't want to come too soon," he said, almost growling. "I want to savor it. I want to savor *you*."

That was it. The sound of him struggling to keep from going over pushed Eva into her climax. She cried out and arched her back as water sloshed against the sides of the tub. Dimly, she could hear Charlie groaning over the phone, and she knew he'd just come, too. She could feel it in her bones. Her fingers twitched, sending more shocks of pleasure through her.

"Oh, God," she said, breathing heavily. "Charlie."

"I'm here," he said, obviously breathless. "You came, didn't you? You came all over your sweet little fingers, like a dirty little girl."

Eva closed her eyes as his words sent a last spark of pleasure through her. "Yes," she said, smoothing her hands down her body. Her pussy ached. The orgasm had been lovely, but nothing like when Charlie made love to her. When Charlie was with her, her body *knew* it. Her pussy felt used after a bout of sex with him. Sometimes it felt abused, and she loved it. She loved the way he made her feel. She loved *him*, God help her. "I wish you were here, though."

"Sweetheart, I wish I was there, too. I'd pick you up and dry you off, and then tuck you into bed with me," he said, sighing. "You'd sleep in my arms all night."

"Sounds nice." She rested her head against the rim of the bathtub, wishing with all her heart that real life wasn't so freaking hard. Her limbs felt heavy and tired. The thought of getting up and out of the tub exhausted her. *You should tell him*, she thought, but didn't. "I'm really sleepy now," she said, instead of coming clean about the baby. It wasn't even a lie. All of her anxiety and confusion of the past few weeks had worn her to bits. Before she could fall asleep and drown, she lifted the drain plug with her toes. "My muscles feel like jelly."

"You should dry off and go to sleep, Eva," Charlie said.

She nodded as the water drained. The chill of the air woke her a little, so she stood up and began to dry off. "I'm getting dressed now."

"Good. I had visions of you slipping under the water and drowning," Charlie said, sounding just as tired as she felt.

Eva pulled on her pajamas. "You should go to sleep, too."

"I will," he promised.

That was good enough for her. Eva didn't even bother brushing her hair as she grabbed her phone and stumbled to her bedroom. She was going to wake up with a gnarled mess on her head, but she was too beat to care. "I'm going to sleep for a week." She got into bed and pulled up the covers, yawning.

"That's not a bad thing. It'll be one week closer to me being home," Charlie said softly. "Dream of me."

"Okay," Eva murmured, eyes closing as she tucked the phone under her pillow. "Love you." If he replied, she couldn't hear him as darkness sucked her down.

****

Charlie lay on the bed, spunk all over his stomach, frozen in place. When Eva had whispered those two words just before disconnecting the call, his heart had nearly burst out of his damned chest. She was sleepy, and he wasn't even sure she realized what she'd said to him, but that just meant it was more likely to be true. To be real. God, he wished he were home, instead of here, dealing with stupid contracts and stupid people.

"I love you, too," he said softly, just to try out the words. The syllables fell into the bleak silence of his lonely hotel room, and he sighed. They weren't at all difficult to say, and that scared the shit out of him. "You're an idiot," he told himself, louder. Those words echoed back at him, and he grimaced.

He'd just realized that for all his worrying about their age difference, it didn't matter. He'd already fallen too hard and too deep to deny the truth. He loved Eva. Even if she ended up pushing him away sometime in the future, she was his woman, and he would be her man for the rest of his life, no matter what happened. He'd never been one for commitment, but he'd fallen hard and fast and hadn't even realized it. And right now, he wished he could hold his woman, and make her feel better, instead of just seducing her into phone sex. More than ever, he realized that Eva was *it*, for him. She was the one.

"And ain't that a kick in the head," he muttered, rolling over to grab a handful of tissues from the nightstand. "After all this time alone, thinking I'd be a bachelor for the rest of my life, I fucking fall for my best friend's daughter. God." He tossed the rolled-up wad of tissues in the direction of the trashcan, not caring that he missed. He needed to get home. He needed to find out why Eva sounded so different lately. Oh, sure, the sex just now was sweet, and he *knew* she'd enjoyed it, but there was something bothering her. Something more than her just being tired from work. He could sense it, and it hurt the way a toothache nagged at a person. Something had her worried, and he needed to find out what it was, and either fix it or help her handle it because that's what you did when you loved someone. He'd learned that from the way Phil cared for his wife and daughter. The same daughter he was now in love with. He had a hell of a lot to live up to.

God, you're an idiot, Charlie, he told himself, staring at the ceiling until he finally realized that sleep was never going to happen when his mind was such a fucking mess. And his heart hurt. Being in love sucked. "Because I can't do anything to help her from two states away." He frowned, then sat up. "Fuck it." He grabbed his phone and shot off a quick text to his cousin.

Charlie: **can you handle the last few supplier interviews without me? I want to head home in the morning**

RJ: **Yeah, no problem. Does this mean you've finally come to your senses?**

Charlie: **I'm not answering that**

RJ: **Uh huh. Give the girl a kiss from me**

Charlie rolled his eyes. Leave it to RJ to know immediately why Charlie was going home. The man had been nagging him about Eva this entire trip.

Charlie: **fuck you, I ain't kissing her for you**

RJ: **buy a ring before you leave, there's a nice jeweler's shop down the road, local metal artist**

Charlie sighed. Of course there was, and of course RJ knew about it. "Saves me from having to look one up, I suppose," he muttered, half annoyed, and half grateful. He pursed his lips, then replied.

Charlie: **yes mother**

RJ: **kiss kiss**

Charlie didn't bother to answer *that*. RJ was an asshole. A useful asshole, but still an asshole. He tossed his phone on the nightstand and shut off the light. For the first time in weeks he felt sleepy. His stomach didn't hurt. Had the answer to his insomnia been so easy all along? *Marry her,* the voice in the back of his head said. That voice sounded suspiciously like Phil, his best friend and Eva's stepdad. It always said the same thing to him, but for the first time he answered:

"I'm going to, Phil. I promise."

Chapter Eleven

Eva took off from work the next day. It was a Thursday, which made taking off problematic, but she couldn't care less at this point. The high from the phone sex with Charlie had long since worn off. She'd woken up that morning feeling completely run down, and something told her that she really needed a day to just get her shit together, if she *could* get her shit together. Life felt insurmountable. She hadn't felt this depressed since the first days after her mother's funeral. Fortunately, most of her morning sickness seemed to have eased up, so she'd spent half the day in bed, staring at her ceiling because she was just too sad to get up. Gravity weighed her down. Gravity weighed her down *hard*.

"Pregnancy hormones suck," she muttered, finally. "You're a grownup. Get out of bed and start acting like one." When she rolled over, the clock on her wall told her it was almost one in the afternoon. She hadn't eaten all day. Why was she so damned depressed? Oh, yeah. She hadn't told Charlie about the baby yet. And she had no idea what the hell she was going to do with an infant.

"But you have to tell him. He deserves to know," she informed herself, sliding out of bed. Once she got herself standing up and halfway mobile, she went into the bathroom and washed her face with cold water, thinking that it would shock her awake if nothing else. It did, sort of, if making herself hate the universe just that tiny bit more counted as waking up. She stared in the mirror. She looked a bit pale, but considering she'd been throwing up every day for almost a month, that wasn't surprising. Thank God that had stopped. She couldn't imagine how women who suffered it for their entire pregnancy functioned at all. "Put on your big girl panties,

Eva," she said, pointing at her reflection. "No one else is going to do it for you."

An hour later she'd managed to eat something, and drink two entire glasses of water. Dehydration was not good for her, or the baby. She felt a little better, but that wasn't saying much. Depression had a way of picking at the psyche until even the simplest things felt impossible. When you had to do something not simple, like inform your boyfriend of an unexpected pregnancy, and you were scared to death of what might happen, life turned grim.

"Just freaking call him," she muttered, staring at the remains of her sandwich. She poked at a crust of bread. "Just do it." But instead of picking up her cell phone, or clearing away her plate, she staggered up and went back to bed, landing face down on the comforter. She was just so freaking *tired*. She'd call him in a minute. Or maybe five.

An hour later, Eva sat up in a tangled mess of sheets and comforter. She put her fingers on her face and prodded. "What the hell," she muttered. Her skin felt weird. She was woozy. She hadn't actually meant to fall asleep again; she was just going to rest for a bit. "I must really need the rest. Maybe I should take tomorrow off, too. Have a long weekend," she mumbled, rubbing her face until it hurt. As anticipated, her hair felt like a snarled rat's nest on the back of her head, and she grimaced. If Charlie showed up right now, he'd run screaming the other direction. *And for more reason than how I look*, she mused grimly.

She sighed, then swung her legs over the side of the bed. She had to pee. And she had to stop moping around like such a loser. She had to be responsible, because she had another life depending on her now. She had so many things she *had* to do, she felt like she was maybe going crazy, but she also just felt numb.

"Which is just … strange. Hmm." For a moment, for the first time since she'd realized that her missing periods were a *thing*, a hint of joy struck her. Having a baby meant she'd have a family again. Even if Charlie wasn't okay with it, she kind of was. Wasn't she? The numbness receded just a bit. She'd missed being part of something bigger than herself. She'd lost her father and then her mom so quickly she hadn't really even finished mourning them. She walked over to her dresser and looked at her mother's picture.

"You would be so happy about this, wouldn't you, Mom?" she asked softly, touching the cool glass. Her mother smiled up at her, and Eva sensed a bright rush of love seep into her. She put her hand on her stomach and smiled. "I'm going to take care of you," she promised her baby. She straightened her spine. It didn't matter that she was scared. It didn't matter that she was depressed, or sick, or any number of other things. She had to think about the future, and that meant talking to Charlie.

"You'll tell him tonight, on the phone," she said, testing out the idea in her head. "And maybe he'll be angry, but so what?" She shuffled to the bathroom. "He's not a violent guy. He's not a jerk. Isn't that why you wanted him to be your first lover? You picked him specifically because you knew he was a good guy." She remembered how resistant he'd been to the idea, and she had to laugh. He'd caved in to her pretty quickly, and then … wow. He'd hadn't just popped her cherry; he'd made love to her over and over again: sweet and hot and amazing. He'd been awesome. He'd been everything she ever wanted. "And he still is, which is the problem, I guess," she murmured. The face looking back at her in the mirror still looked drawn and tired, but her expression had eased a bit.

"You can do this," she told herself, and then she pushed down her pajama pants and sat on the toilet, still grumbling to herself. "Okay, so maybe he really didn't want to be in a permanent relationship, but what man does? Maybe he's just scared. Maybe he'll be okay with the baby," she said as she peed. When she reached for the toilet paper, she frowned, suddenly lightheaded again. "God, what the hell is wrong with me? I must really need to get some sleep." She wiped, and then went to throw out the paper, when a streak of blood caught her eye.

Eva gasped, hands shaking. "No. Oh my God, no!"

****

"Okay. This is it. Think positive, man," Charlie murmured as he let himself into Eva's house, feeling as nervous as a teenage boy on his first date. He quietly shut the door behind him, wondering if Eva was even home. Her car was in her driveway, but sometimes she took the long bus to the city so she didn't have to do the park and ride thing, so that was no guarantee she was inside. He'd spent the day driving down from upstate New York, even though he knew she might not be home from work when he got there. In fact, she probably wasn't, but he couldn't go to his place. He'd wait for her here for the rest of the day if he had to, because he had a ring in his pocket and a question on his mind, and he hoped to God that Eva didn't break his heart. *And if she does, I'll just try again until she realizes that I'm her guy*, he promised himself.

He stepped into her living room, smiling at the scent of strawberry tea. She loved the stuff. He'd forever associate the scent of it with her. When he saw the remains of a lunch on her table, his smile slipped away. Was she home? That was odd. He checked the time on his phone. It really was too early for her to be here.

"Hello? Eva?" he called out, heading for the kitchen. Before he'd taken two steps, a horror filled cry from the bathroom tripped his heart into overdrive. The next thing he knew, he was in the hallway outside of the bathroom, pounding on the door. "Eva! Are you okay?" He was afraid to open the door. The moment he did, nothing would be the same again. Dread squeezed his chest.

"Charlie! Is that you?" Eva cried out, sounding like someone had a hand on her throat. "Help. I need you."

That was all the permission he needed to go through the closed door. He rushed inside and found her sitting on the toilet, clutching a bloody wad of tissues. "Sweetheart?" He went to his knees. His mind raced. Did she get her period? Why would that upset her so much?

"I think I'm losing the baby, Charlie," she sobbed, and he froze, stunned.

Baby? What baby?

"I don't want to lose it." She swiped at her face, rubbing red streaks into her cheeks. "I didn't know how much I wanted it until just now. I thought it was a disaster. I thought you would hate me." She started crying.

Oh my God. A baby, his mind stuttered, even as he gathered her into his arms. He ignored the blood. Eva needed him. "Honey, I'm here. It's going to be okay. Shh, it's okay."

"I didn't know how to tell you," she cried, clutching at his shirt. "I felt so guilty, because I forgot about how antibiotics mess up the pill, and it must have happened almost as soon as we started this thing, whatever this thing is, and I'm so sorry." She looked up at him, face devastated. "I'm so sorry. I know you didn't want to have to deal with something permanent, and I

won't force you to stay, but I don't know what to do."
She cried harder.

Antibiotics mess up the pill? What does that mean? he wondered, but she started gasping for air before he could ask. She was panicking, which meant that he had to keep his shit together. Charlie inhaled, and pushed all his questions to the back of his head. His woman was sick, and distraught, and she needed him. Everything could wait. Right now, he had to take care of her. Somewhere deep inside panic welled up, but he pushed that down, too. He would *not* let himself freak out right now. Eva was going to be okay. He'd make sure of it. "Shh, it's okay, baby," he soothed, grabbing more tissues to wipe her face. He had to clean the blood off. "I'm not mad. I'm here. It's going to be okay. I promise."

She grabbed the tissues from him and scrubbed at her face until it was blotchy. Even upset, she looked adorable. He couldn't believe he'd been so stupid, thinking that he couldn't let himself love her. *What the fuck did you think was going to happen, moron?* he told himself. *Did you think you could just fuck her and then let her go? Ha. Fat chance. This is Eva. Phil's little girl. You've always loved her, you dumbass.*

"It's not a lot of blood, but I don't know what to do," she was saying.

Charlie forced himself to deal with the moment, instead of chasing the terror of what-if in circles around his head. He glanced down at the tissues she'd let fall to the floor. It looked like a hell of a lot of blood to him, but what did he know? He'd never even seen a period in real life before, let alone a miscarriage. He took a deep breath. Now was not the time to be squeamish.

"Do you have a doctor, honey? Is there someone we can call?" Even as he said the words, he wondered if he should just pick her up and take her to the emergency room.

She nodded. "Yeah. I went to see her a few days ago. She said everything looked good, but she was wrong. Obviously." She stared down at the floor sadly. "I even had a sonogram."

I have no idea what that is, he thought, but it didn't matter. He cradled her in his arms, afraid to hold onto her too tightly. She felt so damned fragile to him. So small. "Does your belly hurt? Cramps? Anything?" he asked her.

Eva shook her head. "No. I just feel tired. A little lightheaded, but that might be because I haven't been eating."

"You haven't been eating?" Charlie frowned. Now that he thought about it, she looked like she'd lost weight. And if she was really pregnant, that was bad, wasn't it? "Have you been sick?" He'd read about some women getting morning sickness so bad they couldn't keep anything down. Would Eva have hidden that from him? *Could* she have hidden that? *You went off on a business trip right when she needed you most*, he told himself. Guilt pricked at him. It was an emotion that had become way too familiar.

"Yeah. I was throwing up in the morning and sometimes at night, but that went away the past few days. I thought I was over the worst of it," she said, and then she sighed. "I was more upset about telling you than anything else. I was afraid to tell you."

Charlie pulled her into a hug. That admission just about killed him. Because he'd clearly made her feel as if she couldn't count on him when things got tough. *I'm a selfish bastard,* he thought, wishing he could punch himself in the face for making her feel so lost and alone. *Phil would be livid.* Shame flashed through him, jolting his stomach.

"I'm sorry, Charlie," Eva said again, holding onto him.

"Don't be sorry. You didn't do a damn thing wrong," he said, swallowing hard against the emotion lodged in his throat. She felt so small in his arms, and it struck him all over again how fragile life was. He'd felt it when his brother died, and then again when they'd lost Phil. And now, with Eva so vulnerable and sick… He gritted his teeth, telling himself not to go there. She would be okay. He couldn't imagine a reality where she wasn't.

"I don't know what to do," she said in a small voice.

"It's okay. I'm here. You don't have to figure it out alone," Charlie said, kissing her forehead.

"Okay," she said, shuddering.

Charlie stroked her hair back from her face. "Here's what we're going to do. You're going to pull up your pants and we're going to call your doctor and see what she says." He twisted and rummaged around in the cabinet under the sink until he spotted her sanitary pads. "Here." He grabbed one and helped her peel the paper tabs off the back, revealing the sticky strips that held it secure. "This should tide you over until we can decide what to do." He helped her secure it to her panties. "Now we're going to wash your face so you feel better."

"Okay," she said, agreeing with him too easily as he helped her stand up and rinse her tears away.

That more than anything told Charlie she was too exhausted to think. *I'll just have to do it for her, for now.* He helped her pull her pants on over her panties, and then he brushed her hair into a loose ponytail for her while she called her doctor. He listened to her explain her symptoms as she slumped on top of the toilet seat. He wanted to kick himself all over again for not noticing how unhappy she'd really been the last several weeks. His knees were killing him from the hard tile floor, and the bathroom cabinet door pull dug into his shoulder blade, but he'd crouch here forever if he had to, in order to keep Eva safe. When she finally hung up and looked at him, his heart tripped against his ribcage at the expression on her face.

"She said we should go to the ER."

****

Eva sat in Charlie's truck, feeling like a used-up washcloth—frayed and thin and ready for the trash bin. She wasn't used to feeling so helpless, but she supposed a possible miscarriage was enough to flatten even a superwoman. She rubbed her face again. At this rate, she'd rub all the skin right off and end up looking like a monster.

"Almost there," Charlie said, sounding calm and impossibly reassuring.

"Thanks, Charlie," she said. She wondered when the other shoe would drop. Charlie hadn't said a word about the baby, and he hadn't seemed mad at all, so she didn't have a clue about how he really felt. Was he angry? Sad? Frightened? His calm demeanor told her nothing. She almost felt like screaming at him, but she just couldn't muster up the energy for it.

"I'm going to drop you off and then park in the front lot, okay?" he told her, touching her knee.

Eva nodded. What else could she do?

A half hour later she was in one of the bays in the emergency room, waiting for a portable ultrasound device to be rolled in. Charlie stood next to the bed, holding her hand. "I'm just so sorry, Charlie," she couldn't help saying. Again. As if it would change anything at all. She bit back a sob. The pad in her panties was wet and uncomfortable, and she was terrified to go to the bathroom to check how much she was still bleeding. She rubbed her eyes. The incessant beeping from the other bays hurt her head. Everything about this place triggered bad memories of being with her stepdad and her mother when they were sick. *Doesn't everyone die after being in the hospital?* she mused. *My baby is going to die, too.* She touched her abdomen with her free hand. She couldn't feel anything.

"Eva, honey. Stop. You didn't do anything to be sorry about," Charlie said again, for maybe the thousandth time. "*I'm* the one who's sorry."

Wait, what? She frowned up at him. "What? No. You've always been truthful with me about everything. You told me from the beginning that this wasn't going to be a long-term relationship. I knew that going in."

He just looked at her, and for a moment, she'd swear she saw guilt on his face. That terrified her. She didn't want his guilt. She wanted his *love.*

"Actually, that's not true," Charlie finally said. "I lied about not wanting more than a hookup or a short-term fling." He looked away for a moment. "I was afraid of how I felt about you." He turned back then, and looked her straight in the eyes. "I've always loved you."

Eva nearly stopped breathing. *Wait, what? What did he just say?* But before she could work herself into a frenzy, he sighed and sat down on the bed, resting his forehead on her hand. His skin felt very, very warm. When her turned his head and kissed her fingers, his light brown eyes were blurred with tears.

"I fell in love with you the first moment we made love, Eva," he said, looking at her steadily. "And I knew from then on out that I wouldn't be able to let you go. I knew what we had wasn't going to be just sex. I lied to you because I was lying to myself."

Eva struggled to inhale. She couldn't believe the

words he'd just said. *Am I dreaming?*

Charlie held himself absolutely still, like a man about to leap from the edge of a cliff. "And I was a fool for denying it. I was a fool for never telling you how I felt all the weeks we spent together, and for pretending that it would only ever be about the sex." He shook his head. "I'm an ass, Eva, and I am so very sorry I ever, *ever,* made you feel like you couldn't talk to me." He paused, seeming to gather himself. "About *anything.*" He smiled. "Especially about having a baby. That's just…" Charlie broke off and shook his head. "It's amazing, Eva."

Eva clutched his hand like a lifeline. For so long she'd felt like she was drowning, and now here he was, pulling her up above the water when she least expected it. "I thought you'd be angry," she whispered, feeling tears well up again. "I didn't know what to do. That's why I didn't want to talk to you when you were away. I knew you'd be able to hear it in my voice."

"Angry? No, never. I could never be angry about this." Charlie leaned in and kissed her softly. "I'd be honored to be the father of your child, Eva."

She started crying again. Somehow, he'd said *exactly* what she needed most to hear. "Charlie—" she began, but he put a finger on her lips.

"No, let me talk. I haven't done enough talking, and I regret that, deeply," he told her, voice breaking. He took a deep breath. "If the worst happens, and I'm not saying it will, but if it does, I'll grieve with you." He swallowed, gripping her hand. "And then I'll give you another baby, if you want one. But I hope we don't have to grieve. I hope that this is just a blip on the radar." He gestured to her lap.

Before she could respond, a nurse walked in followed by a tech rolling the portable ultrasound cart.

"Okay, it's time to find out just what's happening here," the nurse said cheerfully as the tech began setting up her equipment.

Eva looked at Charlie and he nodded at her reassuringly, then stood up by the bed. He didn't let go of her hand, and Eva didn't want him to. She clutched it like a lifeline.

"Is this the father?" the nurse asked, glancing at Charlie. "Do you want him to stay in the room with you?"

Eva took a deep breath. For the first time in a long time, even though she had no idea what would happen, she felt just the tiniest bit less terrified of her future. She looked at Charlie only to find him gazing at her steadily, strong and solid. She knew then that she'd always be able to hold onto him, even when the world turned upside down. He was here for her now, when she needed him desperately, and he always would be. She believed in him, because he believed in her.

"Yes, he's the father, and he's staying right here," she said to the nurse, and then she leaned back, ready to find out the future.

Chapter Twelve

Charlie watched Eva sleep in his bed at his house. After the ultrasound tech had done her thing, with the nurse assisting, the OB/GYN on call at the hospital had come in and reassured them both that the bleeding was just a transitory thing. To say he'd been relieved was seriously understating matters. Eva had gone limp in his arms at the news, and he knew then that he'd never let her go again. He only hoped that she would forgive him for being such a stubborn ass these past few months.

"You're mine, sweetheart. You and the little one," he murmured, reassured by her steady breathing. He touched her cheek lightly, then drew her closer when she wrinkled her nose in her sleep. She was adorable. He kissed her nose, and she huffed out a breath in her sleep.

Thank God she's okay, he thought, closing his eyes against her hair. The underlying antiseptic scent of the hospital that clung to her was slowly fading as her warmth pressed her own unique perfume into his bed. He could feel the tension slowly draining out of his body. When the tech had pulled up Eva's paper gown, her softly rounded stomach hadn't looked pregnant. If anything, Eva looked as if she'd *lost* weight, and he'd vowed then and there to take care of Eva properly from now on. She shouldn't have to worry about anything, least of all him and his damned stubbornness, especially when she'd been so sick from carrying their child. *And I didn't even notice,* he thought, angry all over again at his idiocy.

Eva stirred, and he stroked her arm until she settled down again. Surprisingly, it settled him down, too. It felt like a dream that she could be pregnant, and it seemed impossible that he could fall in love with an unborn baby so easily and so quickly, but then he'd seen the little blip on the screen for himself, and that had been it. *Game over.* The tiny bean had a faint heartbeat. He'd even been able to hear it while Eva had sighed and held his hand so tightly he'd lost feeling in his fingers. He couldn't even begin to wrap his head around what it felt like to know that he was going to be a father in a few short months.

"Mmm, Charlie?" Eva said, snuggling closer to him. She opened her eyes, blinking adorably, and then she frowned through a yawn. "Where are we?" She glanced around the dimly lit room.

"I took you home, honey. Don't you remember? You fell asleep in my truck," he said, sliding a hand down her curly, bed mussed hair. "You were exhausted after everything that happened, and the doctor said you needed rest more than anything else right now." He smiled, imagining her ensconced in his house. "No work for a week."

"Home?" Eva looked at him groggily, then glanced around before yawning again. Her curly hair was mashed on one side of her head, and she had a pillow crease down her cheek.

She'd never looked more beautiful to him.

"No worries," he told her, heart so full he thought it might actually burst. "You're safe here." He had to swallow against the ache in his throat. It could so easily have gone badly. She could've died, along with the baby, from any number of terror-inducing problems. He remembered his mother explaining to him how hard pregnancy and birth were on the body, and that was why she'd only had two children. Charlie never thought he'd marry, let alone fall in love and end up having children at all, and now he remembered every word his mother had said. Eva's pregnancy was a surprise, in more ways than one. *But a good surprise,* he thought.

"But this isn't my home." Eva sat up, interrupting his train of thought, and he tucked a pillow behind her back so she could rest against the headboard of his bed. She looked perfect there. She looked perfect in his bed. In this room. He was pleased now that he'd chosen the white faux-leather upholstered bed frame, although when he'd picked it out, he hadn't been sure because he'd thought it was too feminine. He glanced around, wondering what Eva saw. He'd painted the room a soothing sage green, and the furniture was a lovely deep walnut that he'd fallen in love with when he saw it at the warehouse. He hoped she liked it here, but if she didn't, he'd tear everything down and remake it all over again for her. He'd buy, or hell, handcraft whatever she wanted. He'd built the entire house himself, with only minimal help from some contractor friends, and he could unbuild it if he had to. *I'd do anything for her.*

"This is your bedroom, isn't it?" Eva asked him, looking more awake. "It feels like you." She half smiled. "It *smells* like you." She touched the headboard, and then the pillows. "I like it. You chose soothing colors."

"Yes." Charlie smiled. "It's my bedroom. I'm glad you like it." He couldn't stop the giddy feeling rising in his chest. It just felt so good to have her here, in his space. He'd never brought another woman home, and he'd never wanted to, but with Eva, he'd been fighting his instincts for the past two months. He'd known almost immediately that she would look wonderful in his bed, and he hadn't been wrong. Her chestnut hair and soft, pale skin looked divine against his dark green sheets.

Eva stared at him, eyes luminous in the soft light. "What now?"

"You're in my home." He took a deep breath, trying to calm the jitters that had just woken up in his stomach as he contemplated the question he was about to ask her. What if she said no? What if she wanted him to bring her back to her house in town? "And I hope you'll make it yours, too," he finally said, voice low. He couldn't bring himself to speak the words any louder.

Eva stared at him. "Are you asking me to move in?" She seemed shocked. Even after everything that he'd said, her expression told him she was genuinely surprised by his words.

If that surprised her, then this is going to shock her speechless. Charlie steeled himself to get on with the rest of it, then slowly reached into the pocket of his jeans to extract the ring box he'd brought with him from New York, and then to the hospital, and now to his house. Her gaze on him felt wonderful, but also terrifying.

"Charlie?" Her attention was riveted on the box in his hand.

He fingered the soft velvet. "Eva, I'm asking you to marry me." He looked down, feeling suddenly bashful. He had to explain to her that he wasn't proposing just because of the baby. That point seemed urgently relevant. "I bought this in a little shop in upstate New York near the lumber mill I'd gone up there to see. I realized yesterday that I was being unbelievably stupid." He opened the box, showing her the pale pink emerald engagement ring he'd picked out.

Eva gasped, staring at the ring, and he smiled at her stunned expression. The color of the stone reminded him of her blushes, and he knew pink was her favorite color, so when he'd seen the unique gem in a delicate rose gold setting, he'd bought it immediately, despite the hefty price. Eva was worth everything to him. What was a little money when it came to her happiness? "I realized that I was destroying any chance we could have at happiness with my stubbornness," he told her hesitantly. "I hope you'll forgive me."

Eva's gaze flew up to his face. Charlie's heart knocked against his ribcage. Her startling hazel eyes were wide and bright.

God. She's so fucking beautiful. Eva was the only woman who could flatten him with just a look. He slid to his knees beside the bed. "Evangeline Ruston, will you do me the very great honor of becoming my wife?"

****

Eva reached out a trembling hand, and Charlie grasped it. She could feel his hand shake, too, which was almost more shocking than the proposal. *He decided to do this before he knew about the baby,* she realized, and that was the thing that decided her. That and the hints of worry and remorse she could see as she gazed into his eyes. He'd finally figured it out. She saw it in the way he held himself, so still, but filled with nervous energy. She saw it in the way he gripped her hand. She saw it in his heart.

"Eva?" Charlie asked, voice low and soft.

She nodded, gripping his fingers hard. He was her lifeline, after all. "Yes," she said, barely able to get the word out before she burst into tears. "Yes, I'll marry you, Charlie." She gasped as he surged up and pulled her into his arms.

"Thank God," he muttered against her hair. "I don't know what I would've done if you'd said no."

"Why would I say no? I love you. I always have." Eva tried not to cry, but who could blame her? The crush she'd always known she shouldn't indulge in had just culminated in the most epic declaration ever. Charlie loved her! He'd proposed! *I must be dreaming,* she thought, holding onto him as if he were about to vanish in a puff of smoke.

"I love you, too, sweetheart," he told her, arms around her so tight she thought she might not be able to breathe.

She didn't care. *Who needs air?* she thought, tipping her head back to see his face. He seized the moment and kissed her, then leaned back, taking the ring out of the box. *Oh, right. The ring.* She watched, bemused, as he brought it to her hand. It was funny how the piece of jewelry felt so secondary to Charlie's emotional declaration.

"Here," he said, sliding it onto her finger.

She smiled, ignoring the tears streaming down her face. The lovely pink gem winked up at her, and she turned her hand this way and that, letting the light catch it. "It fits perfectly, Charlie. It's so beautiful." She hugged him, crying harder. When she drew back to look at it again, he kissed the palm of her hand, then each fingertip, one by one.

"I hoped it would fit," he said, and she could tell he was smiling by his voice, but she didn't want to tear her eyes away from her ring to make sure.

"I love it. Pink is my favorite color," she whispered. She couldn't have picked out a more perfect ring if she'd chosen it herself. She admired it for a moment longer, then closed her fingers around the band. "You're sure about the baby, too?" Her voice wavered, but she had to ask. She couldn't help it. She'd spent too long worrying about what he was going to do when she finally told him. She needed reassurance. She needed *him.*

"Oh, honey, yes," Charlie said, closing her in his arms again. "I'm happy. I'm so fucking happy. I never thought I'd ever have kids, and I never thought I'd fall in love, and here I am. You've taught me so much. You've given me a family. I haven't had one of those in a long time." He kissed her temple. "I'm sorry I was such an idiot."

His words were all the reassurance she needed. *Well, that and the proposal*, she thought, amused at herself. *A proposal is a very tangible thing when it comes with a ring as expensive as this one looks to be.* She glanced down at it again as happiness spread through her. "It's okay. I never thought this would happen for me, either. I'd never even been on a real date with a man who wanted me, until you," Eva said, cupping his face in her hands. The thought of how many guys had turned her down made her grimace, but Charlie kissed her and she had to grin at his expression. Their age difference didn't feel like anything at all anymore. "Charlie, we're going to get married! And have a baby!" she exclaimed, doing a little wiggle on the bed.

"Yes, we are." Charlie laughed. "So, which one do you want to do first?" He shifted his weight, lying down next to her on the bed. He lifted one of her curls and began to twist it around his finger.

Eva rolled her eyes at the twinkle in his. He already knew what she wanted, the wretch. "I want to get married first, of course. Duh."

"Why am I not surprised." He walked his fingers up her arm, eyes crinkling in the corners with his grin. "You have to take it easy for the next week, though the week after should be good."

Next week? What does that have to do with— Oh. Whoa. Wait a second. She tilted her head as her heart gave a happy thump against her ribcage. "You want to elope? In a week?" The idea thrilled her. She'd always dreaded the idea that she'd have to get married without her parents there to see her, and eloping sort of bypassed the entire huge planned wedding thing.

"Technically, in two weeks, if that's what you want," Charlie told her, kissing the crook of her elbow.

"Yes. Definitely." Eva took his hand and threaded

her fingers through his. "I want to. I want to go to Acadia."

Charlie sat up, clearly surprised. "You want to go to Maine? Not Hawaii or Vegas? We can go anywhere you want, sweetheart."

She shook her head. "Nope. I want to get married on top of a mountain." And, too, she knew how much Charlie liked the outdoors. He'd love it. This way they'd both get their dream wedding.

Charlie laughed. "That sounds amazing."

"It sure does," she murmured, looking at her ring again. *I'm never taking it off,* she thought, tilting it so that it caught the light. Again.

"We'll give you some time to rest, and then, if the doctor says it's okay, we can fly up to Maine," Charlie said, grabbing his phone. "I'll drag RJ with us, and you can ask your friend Kyra, so we have witnesses." He tapped a few icons on his cell, bringing up a calendar.

"Wait, fly? You can fly there?" Eva knew the closest airport to the national park was several hours away. How would flying help them?

He shrugged, as if the logistical nightmare was nothing. "You can fly there if you know the right people. Private charters aren't that difficult to arrange. They land in Bar Harbor. I just checked." He set the phone back down. "I'll text RJ tomorrow."

"Won't that be expensive?" Eva had to ask. She knew Charlie wasn't poor, but a private plane seemed, well, insane. *How can he be so blasé about the expense of something like that? I sure can't!*

Charlie looked at her for a moment, and then he grinned. "You have no idea how much money I have, do you?"

Eva frowned. "I know you like your work, and you're really successful, but building tiny houses doesn't seem like the kind of business that would let you book a private plane on a whim." She couldn't even imagine having that kind of money. She'd never been truly poor, but she knew what it was like to have tight finances. The year after her stepfather died had been particularly rough. "You don't have to do something that's going to mess up your savings, Charlie. I'm perfectly happy driving up there." And, too, she couldn't afford to do something crazy and extravagant. She had another life to look after, now. She put a hand on her stomach.

"There is no way I'm going to subject you to a ten-hour car trip when you're feeling so crappy. You know that New England traffic is a nightmare." Charlie shook his head, still smiling. "As for the money—it's not an issue. I was a partner in a technology investment company. Many of the businesses we invested in went public. I made a lot of money." His smile went crooked. "A *lot* of money. I'm rather wealthy, Eva."

Huh. He must have done all that while I was still a child, she thought, perplexed. All her teen and adult memories were of him building things with his hands. Eva chewed on her bottom lip. "Just how much do you mean by a *lot* of money?" she asked tentatively, almost afraid of the answer.

Charlie inhaled slowly, then let it out again. His expression told her he wasn't sure how she would react. "Eva, I'm worth at least five-hundred million," he said quietly.

Five-hundred million? Eva thought, shocked. Charlie nodded as she stared at him. The tips of her fingers tingled. *I can't even comprehend that number. He has enough money to buy a freaking island!* "I can't even—" she began, and then broke off. She had no idea what to say.

Charlie lifted a shoulder, looking almost

sheepish. "Give or take a few hundred million, that is. The market shifts my income up and down, depending on where I put my investments."

"I ... what?" Eva put a hand to her throat, struggling to say something. "You're rich?" Those words were somehow completely inadequate for what he'd just confessed.

Charlie shook his head slowly, confusing her. "No, I'm not rich, but I *will* be, when you marry me. Material wealth isn't what matters to me. Not anymore. Once you make enough to feed yourself and buy a few luxuries, making money becomes nothing more than a way of keeping score, and I hate living that way. It's why I left the business. I'm not in this life to compete with a crowd of arrogant millionaires." He gripped her hands. "*You* matter to me, Eva. This *child* matters." He gestured to her belly.

Eva felt tears well up again. "W-what?"

"Eva, all the money in the world is meaningless when you have no one to share it with," Charlie said quietly. "And I'm positive you know exactly what I'm talking about."

Her breath caught. She *did* know. She'd lost her mother and her father. The past few years had been astonishingly difficult. "I'd give anything to have my mom and dad at our wedding." Her voice caught as she spoke.

"Oh, sweetheart." Charlie pulled her into a hug. "Me too." He stroked her hair. "I have to believe that they're looking down on us, and happy for us. I fought my feelings for you for a long time, because I was worried I was taking advantage of your innocence." Eva tried to protest, but he shook his head. "No, hear me out. It was hard for me to understand that it was my own fear that was holding me back." He took a deep breath and leaned back. "Your mom and dad would be happy for us. I know it. In here." He touched his chest with his fist.

Eva touched her stomach. Somewhere inside her, a new life was growing. She was ready for a new family. "I want to name our baby after them, Charlie."

"Mary if it's a girl, or Phil if it's a boy," Charlie said, smiling at her. "I'd like that, too."

Eva nodded, crying again. "I'm sorry I'm crying. Stupid pregnancy hormones."

"Oh, darling." Charlie kissed the tip of her nose. "Don't apologize for having emotions." He swept her up into his arms again. "Your heart is what I fell in love with. Never stifle it." He leaned back. "I'm so thankful that our baby is going to have such an awesome mother. You're everything I never even knew I wanted."

"Charlie, I love you." Eva clutched at him, and he held her tightly, murmuring his love in her ear. She fell asleep in his arms. Safe. Happy.

In love.

Epilogue

"Charlie, what on Earth?" Eva asked, arm outstretched to keep her balance. She blinked, not quite sure what was happening. They'd just arrived back at their hotel after a ridiculously romantic mountaintop marriage, and he'd surprised her by detouring her past the room where she thought they were staying. He'd tugged her down the hall of the swanky resort to another elevator. When they'd emerged at the top floor, he'd led her to a door at the end of the hall. When he'd opened it, she'd frozen: hundreds of flower petals formed a path from the door into a gorgeous suite with expansive views of the ocean. "Oh my God," she said, almost hyperventilating. "What is this?"

"What does it look like, darling wife?" Charlie asked, a smirk in his voice.

Eva blinked. "It looks like a florist threw up in here."

He laughed, and then he swung her up into his arms. "It does, doesn't it? I better save you from the petal vomit."

Eva shrieked. "Charlie! Are you crazy?" She struggled, but he didn't budge. The muscles in his arms bunched up hard and solid beneath her. "I'm too heavy for you. You're going to screw up your back," she said, just a tiny bit worried. Charlie was strong, sure, but she did *not* want him too injured to participate in what she hoped would be a fun ending to an already amazing day.

Charlie just snorted. "You're not even close to heavy, Eva. And this is our wedding day." He strode into the suite, stirring up the rose petals as he walked. Their sweet scent brightened the air as he moved.

Eva wanted to protest some more, but she also didn't want him to drop her, so she held herself very still.

Charlie pecked her noisily on the lips almost as if he knew exactly what she was thinking, the dratted man. She wrinkled her nose at him. He laughed, and then he nudged open a set of doors at the far end of the luxurious suite. The ocean crashed below them as he gently set her down on a cushioned chaise lounge. "Beautiful," he said, looking at her. "You're the perfect bride."

Eva blushed. She'd found a lovely pink sundress that had been surprisingly easy to hike in to wear to her mountaintop wedding. Her friend Kyra had surprised her at the end of the hike with a short veil that fastened into her hair with a jeweled comb. The weather had been perfect. A group of other hikers had cheered when they said their vows. All in all, it had been a perfect wedding. RJ had stood with Charlie, and the minister had been a local pastor who'd been delighted to perform the ceremony. Apparently, he was an avid outdoorsman, and had loved the idea of bringing his two favorite things together: ministry and hiking.

"You're too sweet, Charlie," Eva said, smoothing her hands down her dress. The material was silky and light and weirdly comfortable. She felt like a princess. The material even hugged her curves in just the right way to flatter her best features and disguise her worst. She *felt* beautiful today.

"No, *you're* too sweet. I guess I'll just have to eat you up," Charlie said, sliding to his knees.

"Oh God." Eva blushed as he slid his hands up her thighs. Even after all they'd done together, whenever he went down on her, she still felt vaguely embarrassed.

"You know the rules, honey," he murmured, thumbs slipping beneath her panties to stroke her labia. "No shame in this. Unless you're saying no?" He tilted his head at her.

Oh, he's teasing me, damn him. Eva swallowed.

"I'm not saying no." She would never say no to him.

"Good." He leaned in and inhaled. "Mmm. You smell so fucking good."

Eva flushed even hotter. "I'm all sweaty from hiking. I should wash."

"Don't you dare." Charlie sat back and grinned at her. "You smell delicious. I bet you taste even better." He hooked his fingers under her panties and slid them down, taking off her shoes as he went. "So. Gorgeous." He kissed the inside of her knees. "I love your thighs." He cupped her, then slid his hands up to her ass. "I love that you have the perfect handful for me to savor." He gripped her ass and yanked her down the mattress.

Eva squeaked, but he was already between her legs, nosing along her slit.

"Perfect," he murmured, kissing her. His tongue darted out and teased her clit. "And so ready for me." He settled in and focused all of his attention on her bud. "Look how wet you are already."

Eva writhed. Sometimes he teased her until she wanted to scream, and sometimes he got right down to it, like he was right now. Charlie always knew what he was doing. "Oh, God," Eva panted, right at the edge of coming, even though he'd barely gotten started. What *was* it about him?

"You want to come, don't you, baby?" he said, stroking her open with his fingers. He slid one into her pussy, pushing up against her G-spot. "Mm, yeah," he murmured, kissing her clit again.

Eva arched her back. Pleasure sparked down her spine as his tongue magicked her into a climax. She almost didn't know what was happening when he brought her over, but then he kept going, even after she began to come down from the pleasure. "Sensitive," she gasped. "Wait a sec."

"Nope." Charlie chuckled. "You're going to give me another one."

Is he serious? Eva shook her head, legs trembling. "I don't think I can so soon, Charlie."

He licked her anyway, circling her bud with his tongue. "You can. You will." He sucked her clit into his mouth, then bit down.

Eva cried out as her entire body tingled. It almost hurt, and then he did something with his fingers that had her pushing back at him, suddenly needing more.

"I've got you," he murmured, sliding his fingers up to her clit. He teased her until she wanted to scream, and then he abruptly stopped.

"No, don't stop," Eva protested, but then he was back, naked this time. "Dammit, Charlie," she said, gripping the comforter. He loomed over her, six foot four inches of pure male muscle, and she groaned softly. She wanted to run her fingers all over him, and then she wanted to dig in and never let go.

"Off with that pretty dress," he said, sliding it up and over her head. He paused, eyes glittering as he took in her lacy bra. "That's a hell of a sight."

Eva bit her lip, hands automatically going to her belly to hide her roundness, but he pushed her away.

"Oh, no you don't," he said, cupping her abdomen. "You're so fucking beautiful, Eva. Don't hide from me." He slid his warm hands up and took off her bra. Her breasts, tender from pregnancy hormones, bounced free, bigger than ever. "Oh, Jesus," Charlie murmured, fingers going to her nipples. "So damn juicy." He leaned in and suckled one, then the other, until Eva was jerking beneath him, trying to get him to fuck her.

"Please," she said, hips wriggling. He felt huge and strong and hot as hell. He was the only man she'd ever known strong enough to handle her.

"You want something?" he asked, eyes twinkling past his arousal.

Eva scowled. "You know I do."

Charlie leaned down and kissed her. "Hang on to something, honey."

Eva licked her lips. He tasted like her, and if that wasn't a hell of a turn-on, she didn't know what was. She reached up and pressed her hands into his shoulders. "Please, Charlie. I need you so bad."

His smile slid away. "Oh, I'm going to fuck you, Eva. No worries," he said, lifting her up so that her hips were no longer at the edge of the bed. "You're going to feel me in your throat."

Eva's breath hitched when he grabbed himself, stroking a few times. His cock stood out from his body, hard and wet at the tip. She wondered if she'd ever get tired of him, but then she shook her head. *It'll never happen.*

"Ready?" he asked.

Eva nodded, trying to get him to come into her. She dug her heels into his ass, and he smirked, then put the tip of his erection at the entrance to her cunny. "So fucking hot," he muttered.

Eva moaned. He wasn't sliding in. Instead, he used his cock to tease her clit, rubbing over the swollen bud until she thought she'd lose her mind. When his fingers slid back to her ass, then dipped into her forbidden hole, she groaned. How could he make something like that feel so good?

"Oh, yeah. Someday I'm going to fuck you in here, and you're going to go insane with how good it feels," he murmured, sliding his finger in and out.

Eva couldn't speak. She couldn't move. She needed more.

He seemed to sense it. "Yeah, you look so

fucking beautiful like that," he said, rubbing her clit at the same time as he finger-fucked her ass. Just as she was about to crest, he stopped and pushed his cock inside, almost too big to fit. "Oh, fuck," he said, shaking.

Eva writhed as pleasure slammed into her. He'd brought her to the edge and left her hanging, and now his body ground into her clit in just the right way to send her flying. "God!" She threw back her head as he began to fuck her. Every grunt, every hard thrust sent her higher and higher, as though her orgasm was a living thing pressing through her body. She held onto to him with all of her strength, and not only did he not seem to care, he didn't even seem to notice.

"Oh, fuck, Eva," he said, thrusting faster. He put his hands on her shoulders to keep her in place. "Yeah, God. Fuck." He hung his head down on her shoulder, and Eva orgasmed again as he slammed into her, hard and huge. His cock dragged along her sensitive pussy, still swollen with the orgasms he'd already given her.

"Charlie, oh my God, what—" she tried to say, but then he surged into her hard, and she felt his shaft pulse inside her body. She shuddered as, astonishingly, one last climax swept through her. It went on and on, and then just when she thought she'd die if it didn't end, Charlie collapsed on top of her, wringing the last shreds of pleasure out of her body. She clung to him with arms and legs wrapped around his strength. She never wanted to let go.

If I wasn't already pregnant, that would definitely have done it, she thought several long minutes later, and then she giggled aloud.

Charlie smiled against her neck, then peeled himself off her and slid to the side. "What's so funny?" he asked, kissing her shoulder.

"I think you may have just gotten me pregnant

again," she said, still laughing.

Charlie snorted, eyes twinkling. "You're lucky I like big families, then." He leaned up, smiling at her. His hair stuck out in all directions.

Eva twined her hands through the strands, smoothing them down. "You're my husband," she said, still marveling over that fact. She never thought they'd get here. She'd resigned herself to a lifetime without him.

"And you're my wife. Forever and ever," Charlie murmured, kissing her softly. "Darling Eva."

"Forever," she repeated, sighing. She closed her eyes, imagining the future. For the first time in years, she wasn't worried. She wasn't lonely.

Charlie put his hand on her abdomen. "I had no idea how much I needed you, Eva." He leaned up and kissed her shoulder. "Thank you for propositioning me." He grinned. "I'm glad you asked me to pop your cherry."

Idiot, Eva thought, rolling her eyes. "If you hadn't been so stubborn, I wouldn't have had to resort to propositioning you." Eva poked his shoulder. "I've had a crush on you since I was twelve, you know."

"I know," he said, and then he shrugged, as if it wasn't a big deal. "Men are stupid."

True story. Eva laughed. "But useful." She paused, pretending to think. "Occasionally."

"Hey! I resemble that remark," Charlie said, laughing.

Eva smiled, then giggled when he tickled her stomach with his stubble. "Stop that." She pushed him away. She was *really* sweaty and gross now. "I need a bath." She tilted her head and sniffed lightly. "So do you."

"I do not." Charlie made a great show of sniffing his armpit.

Eva made gagging sounds, and Charlie laughed

again.

"You're not smelly, Eva. You're perfect." Charlie kissed her hip, and then her stomach. "And so are you, little one," he said, kissing her stomach.

Eva's smile melted away as the look of utter tenderness and devotion on Charlie's face struck her right in the heart. "Oh, Charlie," she whispered, eyes blurry. "I love you."

Charlie looked up. His light eyes pinned her to the bed, somehow hot and sweet and tender all at the same time. "And I love you, Evangelina Ruston Greenwood." He lifted her hand and kissed her wedding band. "Now and forever, for however long that may be."

"As long as forever." Eva smiled at him, ignoring the tears rolling down her cheeks.

Charlie gathered her up into her arms, and she forgot about being sweaty and dirty and fat. She forgot about being alone. She forgot about being afraid. She didn't need to think about any of that anymore, because she had a family to take care of. A family to love.

She had Charlie, and she knew he would walk through fire and back again for her and their baby.

She had forever, and that was a hell of a long time.

The End

www.erinmleaf.com

HOW LONG IS FOREVER?

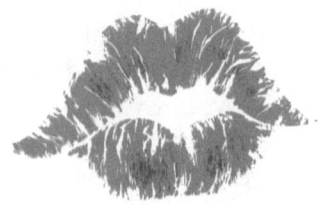

EVERNIGHT PUBLISHING ®

www.evernightpublishing.com